Miss Knight and Others

ROBERT McALMON

FOREWORD BY GORE VIDAL

EDITED WITH AN INTRODUCTION BY EDWARD N. S. LORUSSO

and *Others*

UNIVERSITY OF NEW MEXICO PRESS · ALBUQUERQUE

Library of Congress Cataloging-in-Publication Data
McAlmon, Robert, 1896–1956.
Miss Knight and others / Robert McAlmon: foreword by
Gore Vidal ; edited with an introduction by
Edward N. S. Lorusso.
p.   cm.
"Books of Robert McAlmon": p.
Contents: Miss Knight—Distinguished air—
The lodging house—The indefinite huntress.
ISBN 0-8263-1353-1
I. Lorusso, Edward N. S.   II. Title.
PS3525.A1143M58   1992
813'.52—dc20   92-4323   CIP

Contents

Acknowledgments

For the publication of this book I am much indebted to several people for their interest, encouragement, and prodding. Beth Hadas, Phil Perkins, and Gayle Creighton never faltered in their good humor and good advice. I appreciate their input. And special thanks go to Gore Vidal for graciously helping us to reclaim Robert McAlmon. To all, thanks.

To Phil and Gayle

Foreword

GORE VIDAL

What is one to do—if anything—about Robert McAlmon? He was little known as a writer in his lifetime (1896–1956), and he is now no more than a footnote to twentieth-century literature. Is he a lost master whose works need only to be exhumed for him to be widely read, as happened recently in the case of Dawn Powell? I doubt it. The poetry is slight when placed beside that of his friend and admirer Ezra Pound. The novella *Village* has a certain charm, but placed beside Sherwood Anderson. . . . Of course it is not necessary to place any book beside any other book. It is enough to take it as it is and see what is there. So let us ponder what McAlmon did do.

In McAlmon's lifetime only one book was published in the United States: *Not Alone Lost* (1937), a book of poems. *Being Geniuses Together*, a memoir, was published in England (1938). Later, in 1968, McAlmon's friend Kay Boyle redid the book for American publication, alternating chapters of her autobiography with his. The result illuminated most charmingly the literary life of the American "expatriate" writers of the twenties.

McAlmon was born in Kansas, raised in South Dakota, became an artist's model in New York, wrote poetry and prose; he married a rich woman who liked her own sex as he liked his and with this marriage of inconvenience to support him and free her from her family, the unlikely couple set forth to be geniuses together in Europe in the twenties. She wrote novels as Bryher. He wrote proto-Hemingway sketches of American low life and proto-Pound verse.

In Paris, McAlmon set himself up as a publisher. Whatever the limitations of his own work, he had a sharp eye for genius in others. He published, often first, Gertrude Stein, Djuna Barnes, Ernest Hemingway, and Nathanael West. He gave James Joyce a monthly allowance which was deeply resented by that genius who, in the great tradition, bit the hand that had fed him when he later dismissed McAlmon's memoir as "the office boy's revenge."

Then as now American men were hysterical on the subject of homosexuality. American writers, who tend to be sissies anyway—nose-in-a-book all the time—are even more hysterical on the subject than realtors or arbitragers. McAlmon was not particularly open about his sex life but everyone *knew,* and he was treated with some disdain by Hemingway and Fitzgerald, two sissies in terror of being thought fairies. Whether they were or not is immaterial; many people thought they were (and perhaps they did, too), including a couple of their wives. Certainly McAlmon did and, in his cups, he felt it his duty to reveal Ernest and Scott as fairies. There survive some wonderfully comic letters in which the outraged Scott and

Ernest vent their loathing of McAlmon and his hideous allegations. After all, they wanted to be Great Writers, and every American knew then as they know now that no Great Writer can be a fag: except maybe if he is a European or a Japanese and so it doesn't really count.

McAlmon also did the unforgivable: he gave away certain secrets of the male lodge. In these pages, he is blunt in his portrayal of American fairies in Berlin after the First War—"Grim Fairy Tales," he calls them. But Berlin is Berlin and fairies are fairies—exotic marginal creatures. In the novella *Village* (1924), however, McAlmon described healthy All-American midwestern boys, and he got rather closer than anyone else ever had to revealing what it was that Tom and Huck and Jim had been up to in the previous century; what, indeed, they are always up to, in a casual way—just messing around as we called it in the army during the Second War. No big deal unless someone gives the game away.

In shape and tone, *Village* resembles Anderson's *Winesburg, Ohio*, published a few years before. The novel—a series of sketches, really—is about a place and what time does to the ordinary lives of those who live there. The subtitle: "As It Happened Through a Fifteen-Year Period." McAlmon calls his village Wentworth, North Dakota. Actually it was Madison, South Dakota. The sensitive adolescent protagonist (himself) is one Peter Reynalds, and he is in love with a high school football hero called Eugene Collins, who is actually Eugene L. Vidal, my father. In real life, with another army flyer from the 1917 war, Gene Vidal started the first transcontinental airline. The partner was Paul Collins. Hence, Eugene Collins. McAlmon never let up.

I can testify at first hand that, as far as my family goes,

McAlmon invents nothing. He is a literal recorder. There is my lecherous great-grandfather, whom he calls "the gay rakish Mr. Dubois," a widower always on the lookout for rich widows. There is my grandmother, who was so fat that my father never allowed her to visit him at West Point or, later, come to Washington, where he was Director of Air Commerce. McAlmon notes that she is again pregnant at fifty, as indeed she was, to her horror. My Aunt Lorene is called Loraine, Aunt Emma becomes Renee, and the family's sense of fallen grandeur is captured, particularly the endless discussions of how rich the Vidals would be once the Spanish government paid its debt to them for having raised a Swiss regiment to fight for the Spanish king in the war against Napoleon. To everyone's amazement, just before the Spanish republic fell in 1937, they discharged their debt to us; my father's share was about $100.

Over fifteen years Gene is observed at different angles by Peter Reynalds. He is shown as an athlete, a West Point cadet, an All-American football player, a husband of the "wealthy" [*sic*] daughter of a U.S. senator. What begins as a passion on Peter's side turns to indifference and then dislike as such relations do when one partner, if that is not too strong a word, is quite unaware of the other's adhesion. Finally, Peter notes that Gene's beauty is flawed by too short a neck. This was true, well observed, and revelatory—of the observer.

In the novel *The City and the Pillar* (1948), I made use of precisely the same relationship between two village boys. One takes seriously their messing around while the other forgets all about it as he grows up and goes away and settles into "heterosexuality," an American invention on the order of cellophane. Needless to say, *Village* has all

sorts of reverberations and resonances for me. Certainly
it is a very odd thing to encounter one's father at the age
of fifteen, using a Ouija board to find out if he'll be appointed to West Point or to Annapolis. It also explains
his curious response to a journalist who asked him if he
wasn't disgusted, as any decent person must be, by *The
City and the Pillar.* "Well, no," he said in his South Dakota
drawl. "I wasn't disgusted at all. Personally, I thought it
was very interesting." My father was long dead by the
time I read *Village* a year ago. I just asked my aunt about
McAlmon. "The name's familiar." Nothing more.

Distinguished Air (Grim Fairy Tales) was published in
1925 by McAlmon's Contact Editions, Paris. Three short
stories ("Miss Knight," "Distinguished Air," and "The
Lodging House") set in post–World War I Berlin, a decade
before Isherwood came to town with much the same pre-
occupations as McAlmon except, as far as I recall, there
is little drug-taking in Isherwood's set. Nothing much
happens in McAlmon's stories. The characters, many of
them American, have come to Berlin to have a good time
with boys and drugs. After a while, hangover sets in and
they can't wait to leave town. McAlmon's ear for dialogue
is good but unselective. The characters just keep talking,
and we learn a lot of period fairy jargon. The flat mono-
chromatic style that suits "the wild and dreary plains" of
South Dakota doesn't quite capture what is meant to be a
very daring look at honest-to-God decadence.

To the three stories there has now been added a fourth,
"The Indefinite Huntress," a story that one can place quite
comfortably beside any of Sherwood Anderson's plain
tales of that day. McAlmon has managed to compress an
entire novel in the smallest space possible. Here is an ex-
emplary minimalist novel long before that mini-vogue. A

small midwestern town, an impromptu, almost random, marriage between two people not meant for each other, a Gide-ian *acte gratuite* as a result, perhaps, of a shared passion for a beautiful youth that neither does anything about. In less than thirty pages we get the lifetime of a marriage. The result is satisfying and the concentration of effect and tone like nothing else of McAlmon's that I have read. What is it about? Read and find out. Clue: elective affinities, what else? Along with boys and coke, there was Goethe in the Weimar republic.

Introduction

EDWARD N. S. LORUSSO

This collection contains four of Robert McAlmon's best short stories: "Miss Knight," "The
Lodging House," "Distinguished Air," and
"The Indefinite Huntress." The first three take
place in Berlin around 1920; in the last, McAlmon returns to his roots in the American
Midwest.

McAlmon was very much a product of the
Midwest. He was born in Clifton, Kansas, in
1896 and grew up in Minnesota and the Dako-
tas. Many of his short stories (and his novel,
Village) recount his memories of the wild prai-
ries and the spare people who lived there. In
tone, his prairie stories are similar to those of
Willa Cather and Conrad Richter. Lily Root,
the heroine of "The Indefinite Huntress" is a
"lump of a girl" who stands six feet tall. Inar-
ticulate as she is, Lily cannot put words to the
feelings she has, but she knows she is not interested in her husband, Red Neill, who, in turn,
is jealous of the attention Lily lavishes on her
horses, but cannot articulate his feelings either.

And neither one can put a finger on his/her feelings for twelve-year-old Dionisio Granger, the boy who brings them "together."

This theme of being unable to express feelings or to think them out runs through the story. Both the inability to rationalize and the feeling that they are all caught in a web of some kind mark Lily, Red, and Dion as mythic characters playing out predestined roles. Dion is youthful innocence, unaware of the passions that surround him; Red is constantly frustrated in his feeble attempts to figure out his emotional commitments to Lily and Dion; and Lily, who is always alert to her dislike of people (particularly men) and her not fitting in, finally finds someone who needs her for something other than her managerial abilities.

The parallels to myth are deliberate. McAlmon has rewritten the Greek myths of Artemis, Actaeon, and Dionysus in an American vein.

Lily is a huntress, as the story's title suggests, but more important, she is indefinite (a key word here) until the end of the story, when she finds a suitable prey. In remodeling the myth of Artemis (also known as Diana), McAlmon retains many of the original's characteristics. Lily is of amazonian stature, is virginal, dislikes men, and when we first encounter her she is fresh from the hunt with a string of ducks tossed over her shoulder. The hunting theme runs throughout the story. Lily is also unworldly in two senses of the word: she is not schooled in sophisticated ways; she is not comfortable anywhere on earth. Lily is restless on the farm, cannot live in the nearby town of Lansing, and dislikes big cities like New York.

Red also notices Lily's otherworldly quality: "He didn't understand Lily. She kept changing before him." At another moment, Red is the victim of Lily's hunting prowess: "he was taut in her grasp, and curiously hunted in his expression." Red is clearly prey that Lily has caught but does not want because she is indefinite. And despite Red's size and strength, we are told that Lily is stronger than he is.

Red Neill is the Actaeon figure. In mythology, Actaeon is a great hunter who happens on Artemis as she is bathing. The goddess is so upset by the intrusion that she turns Actaeon into a stag that is torn apart by the hunter's own dogs. Nothing this violent happens to Red, but he does become so listless that even his favorite pastime, hunting, loses all its appeal. In both the myth and McAlmon's story, the Artemis figure is responsible for the death of the Actaeon figure.

The inexpressive Red Neill, the drifter who settles in Lansing and becomes a successful businessman, falls into marriage with Lily, even though he continually tells himself she is not the kind of woman he wants. Red is not even sure he wants to be married, and his hunch proves right: he is unhappy and sexually unfulfilled in his union with Lily. Red becomes lazy and more inclined to drink whiskey. It is as if his strength and vitality are sapped by Lily. And as he grows weaker, finally succumbing to pneumonia, Lily grows stronger. As in the Greek myth, Red is powerless in Lily's grasp and falls prey to her strength.

And what of Dion? The beautiful youth who attracts both Red and Lily seems blithely unaware of his effect on others. Patterned after the myth of Dionysus, Dion represents the duality of human nature (symbolized in the myth by the grape); he elicits both joy and pain in those he touches. He intoxicates Lily and Red. Red is confounded by his yearning to touch the boy during a duck hunting trip and cannot keep his hands off him. Lily admits to twice planning to kidnap Dion; she tells Red that the boy satisfies her "arm hunger."

Beyond his youthful beauty and innocence, Dion is not much of a presence in this story; he doesn't need to be. He serves as a catalyst to stir the unknown desires that lie within Lily and Red, and he is not present during most of the story's major events. In the best tradition of Cather and Richter, Dion, the beloved boy-about-town, goes off to college, only to make occasional visits to the ever-changing hometown.

"The Indefinite Huntress" is more, however, than a story of thwarted lives on the prairie or a clever recasting of Greek myths. Surely it is also the story of Robert McAlmon's own marriage to Winifred Ellerman, known as Bryher.

If McAlmon is Red, Bryher is Lily, and Hilda Doolittle is cousin Helga; Dion reverts to his true Greek character, alcoholic excess. Prior to moving to New York in 1919, McAlmon was not an active drinker and probably did not indulge in homosexual acts, but he was confused about such issues. Like Red, McAlmon went about the business of being successful. Just as Lily comments on Red's beauty and fine body, McAlmon also documents his fine appearance in the short novel, *Post-Adolescence*, in which he describes his own beauty and career as an artist's model.

Bryher proposed marriage to McAlmon just as Lily broaches the subject with Red. And like the fictional marriage, the real-life union between McAlmon and Bryher was one of convenience. Where Lily and Red are brought together by Dion, McAlmon was lured into marriage with Bryher by her money; he could not resist the easy life of money and travel that marriage to Bryher offered.

And although McAlmon often defended his marriage by claiming he had been duped, he did not (apparently) hesitate to accept a large cash divorce settlement.

Bryher fits nicely as a model for Lily. Both women enter into marriage specifically to free themselves from the societal bonds placed on single women. Bryher wanted to free herself from her moneyed father by becoming Mrs. McAlmon; Lily wants to be free to manage her own farm and stock. And both women eventually end up with another woman: Bryher was a long-time companion of the American poet, Hilda Doolittle (known as HD); Lily winds up with her cousin Helga.

McAlmon foreshadows Lily's eventual spiritual bonding with Helga in the opening of the story: Helga fondles Lily's beautiful hair (eventually taking a lock of it) and says "If you ever feel that way, let me know and I'll come and take care of you. . . ." The scene between the two women is strongly erotic as Helga brushes and strokes Lily's hair while Lily strokes Helga's arm. A bond exists here before Red comes on the scene. In real life, Bryher and HD were already a couple when McAlmon met them. In both cases, the heterosexual unions are doomed because of the true natures of the principals.

How does the story of Actaeon/Red parallel McAlmon's own life with Bryher? His reputation suffered (he was dubbed "McAlimony"), and his alcoholic excesses shortened his life. Bryher and her money made it all the easier for McAlmon to succumb to these temptations. She is as responsible for McAlmon's failure as Lily is for Red's death. In pursuing his lifelong dream of being a writer, McAlmon only aggravated all the conditions that existed to preclude his success.

In all three instances, the "hero" is killed by the very

thing he desires most or takes great pride in: Actaeon by his own dogs; Red by his own listlessness; McAlmon by his alcoholic excesses. And Artemis, Lily, and Bryher all share several traits. Although it is unusual for McAlmon to draw on classical literature in his writing, the parallels are too numerous and obvious to ignore. And although Gore Vidal states that McAlmon invents nothing, his stories are never mere retellings of actual events and people; often there is a purposely obscured reason for telling the story.

McAlmon's Berlin stories, "Miss Knight," "Distinguished Air," and "The Lodging House" were previously published in a 1925 collection entitled *Distinguished Air* and subtitled *Grim Fairy Tales*, published by McAlmon in a very limited quantity (115 copies). The same stories were reprinted in the 1960s as *There Was a Rustle of Black Silk Stockings* in an attempt to cash in on their sexual frankness, an attempt that apparently failed.

The stories predate better known works that also deal with post–World War I Berlin and the nightlife there. Christopher Isherwood's well-known *Berlin Stories*, which became the play and film, *I Am a Camera*, which became the stage musical and film, *Cabaret*, appeared in 1935. In comparison to McAlmon's stories, the Isherwood material is tame. It does capture the sense of despair that was rampant in Berlin, but the characters have been cleaned up for mass consumption.

Nightwood, by Djuna Barnes also appeared in 1935. Although T. S. Eliot championed this effort to portray the decadence of Berlin society as a symptom for universal postwar malaise, it has remained only a minor classic. Barnes's perverse Dr. O'Connor is based on the same person as McAlmon's Miss Knight. But it is only in

Djuna Barnes's drawing of Dan Mahoney as Matthew O'Connor first appeared in her novel Ryder. *Reproduced courtesy of Special Collections, University of Maryland at College Park Libraries.*

McAlmon's story that the Miss Knight/Dr. O'Connor character comes alive. Miss Knight jumps off the page as an outrageously comic figure, one lost in a sea of drugs and alcohol and sexual perversion, whose very "abnormalities" make him a better person than the "normal" people around him. At least he is honest.

And because Miss Knight is totally honest about all aspects of his life, he perpetuates none of the polite lies associated with acceptable society. In fact, Miss Knight hates all "refinement." He constantly displays his rough edges, whether he is in a bar, on the stage, or giving a misbegotten Thanksgiving Day feast dressed in an outrageously beaded dress and aigrette. His true nature is never long submerged; he is never a whole person unless he can camp or shriek across a crowded room. In the scene where Miss Knight is sitting with strangers, the air of discomfort is palpable as he stifles his tendencies. Miss Knight finally erupts into the flaming queen he is, and all the stuffiness of polite society is blown away by the volcanic blast.

Miss Knight is a breakthrough character in American literature because he never apologizes for his differences, nor does he camp only in private (as Dr. O'Connor does), nor does he see the error of his ways as Radclyffe Hall's infamous lesbian, Stephen Gordon, does in *The Well of Loneliness*. Miss Knight simply is.

This remarkably frank portrait outshines Dr. O'Connor (in *Nightwood*) despite Andrew Field's claim in his biography of Djuna Barnes that "[O'Connor] has long philosophical monologues. . . . He swoops into matters of myth and history. . . . The Matthew O'Connor of *Nightwood* is a great character, of Shakespearean stature and certainly one of the most memorable literary characters of our century." McAlmon's Miss Knight, however, is much closer to the real-life character, Dan Mahoney, and even Field states that Miss Knight "hates refinement most of all and always speaks in an aggressively rough American way." Field goes on to say that "McAlmon's queen uses several of the stock Mahoney coarse phrases invariably recounted by anyone who ever watched him in action in the cafes."

Barnes has O'Connor say things like, "Death I imagine will be pardoned by the same identification; we all carry about with us the house of death, the skeleton, but unlike the turtle our safety is inside, our danger out." This is a very far cry from McAlmon's Miss Knight.

McAlmon commented on the grandly stilted style Barnes chose for O'Connor: "She has a well-known character floundering in the torments of soul-probing and fake philosophies, and he just shouldn't. The actual person [Dan Mahoney] doubtlessly suffered enough without having added to his character this unbelievable dipping into the deeper meanings. Drawn as a wildly ribald and often broadly funny comic, he would have emerged more impressively." And to prove it, that's just how McAlmon wrote "Miss Knight."

McAlmon's portrait is also much more honest. Dan Mahoney earned his living by performing illegal abortions (he performed one on Barnes) and lived in a bordello in Paris. And although Field dismisses McAlmon's characterization as mere transcription, he eventually admits that "the figure of O'Connor is indeed Mahoney, but the *words* and *tone* and *substance* of what O'Connor says belong solely to Barnes" [emphasis his].

Mere transcription aside, McAlmon does not dwell on the negative acts of Mahoney; instead, he centers his story, "Miss Knight," on the personality of Mahoney and uses this to create a composite type prevalent in 1920s Berlin. In McAlmon's story, Miss Knight is not an abortionist, and although McAlmon does not mask the drug and sexual activities of Miss Knight, we are not forced (or privileged, as the case may be) to witness these acts. Miss Knight is seen at home and in bars and cafes, and McAlmon uses this outlandish character to demonstrate a society out of control. No other character in the story, even those who are straight and drug free, is more appealing than Miss Knight.

It is McAlmon's achievement that Miss Knight does not come across as sordid or evil; rather, he appears to be adrift in an alien, corrupt society where his very eccentricities allow him to live. The reader feels sympathy for Miss Knight; readers would be hard pressed to sympathize with Dr. O'Connor. McAlmon's character is oddly humorous and, despite the obvious strangeness, an honest American type.

When one thinks of the homosexual characters in American or British fiction, those that are openly gay or obviously repressed, one does not usually imagine anyone like Miss Knight. There are Saki's fey British men who tag along in polite society, usually in the company of an aged Countess or Duchess. They are invariably pretty and witty, dropping insults and asides alike with gleeful venom. But there is nothing overtly sexual about them; they are eunuchs. Oscar Wilde's gay men are usually repressed creatures (think of *The Importance of Being Ernest*) for whom sex is never an issue. Of course it was long customary to disguise gay men in literature (all those Tennessee Williams "heroines" come to mind) as something else because the public wouldn't tolerate them in mainstream fiction.

McAlmon did not need to consider the public's tolerance because he published his own material. He could (and did) write honestly and openly about any topic without fear of editorial intrusion or refusal of publication. There was, however, a down side to this nose thumbing: he never got an American publisher in his lifetime and most of his Contact books were banned from entry into this country. And so, despite talent, connections, and the guts to write about life, McAlmon became a forgotten, unpublished writer before he was forty.

Also appearing in this collection is "The Lodging House," a story that deals with lesbians. Harold Files (the

McAlmon character in this story) rents a room in Berlin and becomes friendly with neighboring lesbians who take him on a tour of Berlin's bars. This is probably based on a real-life experience and McAlmon was certainly no stranger to lesbians; he was friendly with some of the leading lesbians of the day: Gertrude Stein, Natalie Barney, Sylvia Beach, Adrienne Monnier, Romaine Brooks, Jane Heap, Thelma Wood, and so on. And of course he was on intimate, if not always friendly, terms with Bryher and HD.

As in "Miss Knight" the characters in "The Lodging House" are not berated for being different. Harold accompanies them on their night journey and describes the events in simple language. Harold is not shocked. One of the lesbians threateningly brushes aside all objections to Harold's entering the lesbian bar and he (and we) get a bird's-eye view: "The room was full of mannish-looking, or at least mannishly groomed women, except the word 'groomed' could not be used on people who looked as the ones in this room did."

The lesbian who admits Harold into this underworld is named Steve. McAlmon's Steve predates Radclyffe Hall's Stephen in *The Well of Loneliness* by several years. Steve is neither witty nor terribly social. All she wants to do is drink cognac and whiskey and snort coke. She is belligerent, threatening to "knock for a goal" the porter at the lesbian bar, and she sharply dismisses one girl as a "German bitch." Steve is not much competition for Miss Knight. The latter is a better-drawn, more interesting character. But still, the lesbians in "The Lodging House" are presented in a clear-eyed, honest fashion.

The last story in this collection, "Distinguished Air," details a night on the town—the town being Berlin. This night too is populated with homosexuals and addicts of every kind and the references to cocaine abound. Foster Graham, whose "every garment had a *chichi* touch," leads the McAlmon character about town. They run into Carrol Timmons, McAlmon's second version of Marsden Hartley (he also appears in *Post-Adolescence*), whose "elderly aunt-like visage did not particularly please." They meet a cartoonist and his girl friend, and the group goes on an all-night binge that ends with the morning sun and breakfast at the O-la-la. Our tour of Berlin night-life is complete with booze and cocaine (references to which are astonishingly contemporary) and a colorful group of revelers. Again, the portrait painted by McAlmon is bleak, perhaps sad, but completely honest.

In fact, McAlmon put it best when he said about these stories that they are "a stark and sharp representation of a type new to literature but not to life. All of the stories in the book deal with variant types with complete objectivity, not intent on their 'souls' and not distressed with their 'morals.'"

Let's hope that today's wise world is ready for McAlmon's guts and honesty. After all, nearly seventy years have passed since he shocked his small world with his candor and sealed his own fate in the bargain. Our society has grown up quite a lot in the last generation; maybe today's reader is adult enough to appreciate McAlmon's "type new to literature but not to life." I hope so.

Ed Lorusso
Albuquerque
August 1991

A Note on the Editing

Although McAlmon's books were plagued by poor typesetting and careless proofreading, which resulted in books with far too many typographical errors, the editing of this collection has been kept to a minimum in order to maintain, as much as possible, the original flavor of McAlmon's writing. Obvious misspellings and typos have been corrected; some punctuation has been standardized; only in a few places have I eliminated superfluous punctuation in order to make a passage read more clearly.

E. N. S. L.

The Books of Robert McAlmon

Explorations. London: The Egoist Press, 1921

A Hasty Bunch. Paris: Contact, 1922

A Companion Volume. Paris: Contact, 1923

Post-Adolescence. Paris: Contact, 1923

Village. Paris: Contact, 1924. Reissued 1990,
   University of New Mexico Press

Distinguished Air. Paris: Contact Editions at
   Three Mountains Press, 1925

The Portrait of a Generation. Paris: Contact, 1926

North America, Continent of Conjecture. Paris:
   Contact, 1929

The Indefinite Huntress and Other Stories. Paris:
   Crosby Continental Editions, 1932

Not Alone Lost. Norfolk, Conn.: New
   Directions, 1937

Being Geniuses Together. London: Secker and
   Warburg, 1938

McAlmon and the Lost Generation. ed. Robert E.
   Knoll. Lincoln: University of Nebraska
   Press, 1962

There Was a Rustle of Black Silk Stockings. New
   York: Belmont, 1963

Being Geniuses Together. Revised by Kay Boyle.
Garden City: Doubleday & Co., 1968
Post-Adolescence: A Selection of Short Fiction.
Albuquerque: University of New Mexico
Press, 1991.

Books Published by Contact Publishing

1922
A Hasty Bunch by Robert McAlmon

1923
A Companion Volume by Robert McAlmon
Post-Adolescence by Robert McAlmon
Two Selves by Bryher
Lunar Baedeker by Mina Loy
Three Stories and Ten Poems by Ernest
    Hemingway
Twenty-five Poems by Marsden Hartley
Spring and All by William Carlos Williams

1924
Village by Robert McAlmon

1925
Contact Edition of Contemporary Writers
Ashe of Rings by Mary Butts
My First Thirty Years by Gertrude Beasley
A Hurried Man by Emanuel Carnevali
The Making of Americans by Gertrude Stein

1926
Palimpsest by H.D.
The Portrait of a Generation by Robert
    McAlmon
The Eater of Darkness by Robert M. Coates
Ladies Almanack by Djuna Barnes

1929
North America, Continent of Conjecture by Robert
    McAlmon
Sailors Don't Care by Edwin Lanham
Quaint Tales of the Samurai by Saikaku Ibara, tr.
    Ken Sato

1931
The Dream Life of Balso Snell by
    Nathanael West

iss

night

With her it was "now I'm tellin' you, Mary," or "now when these bitches get elegant I lay 'em out stinkin'," many times a day, if her mood was a vital one. Apparently he, to the outside world of acute observation, she would hastily apologize had she used the Mary phrase on a man who did not know her well, or who might resent queerness and undue familiarity. "Just a way I talk, yuh know," she would explain in a conciliatory tone. But in a group of sister bitches she had few thoughts but to see that none of them rose above the proper clan manner in elegance without being "raised proper." "I'm so glad I'm a real man," she shrieked across the room or café every now and then to relieve the tension of ennui that might, and does, settle upon all atmospheres at times. Properly she believed herself appointed as a camping comedian, ready to earn a right to her presence by keeping undue seriousness from making dullness exist through an overlong period.

If a man in uniform, a policeman, soldier, or young cadet, passed her gaze she would call out to or after him unless the uniformed man's face was an austere one. "Come, get your supper, dearie, now come on," she'd comment, while jerking her head coquettishly.

"I was talkin' to a guy—one of these here highbrows, you get me, just scientifically interested and all that, you know—and he sez to me, 'did you get queer in the army?' and I sez to him, 'my god Mary, I've been queer since before you wore diddies.' I wuz on to that guy too; trying to pass off as a real man. He's one of them kind that tell you they're real men until they get into bed with you, and then they sez, 'O dearie, I forgot, I'm queer.' Whoops dearie! What us bitches will do when we draw the veil. Just lift up our skirts and scream." Miss Knight was hold-

ing forth when an American brother in sisterhood came
into the Berlin bitchery that many travellers slummed in
through the two years after the great war. Miss Knight
had already given the new-comer a careless onceover, and
then recognition dawned upon her face and she whooped
out, "Well, lookie who's here. If it ain't Miss Collins.
And her and me used to be together in the chorus in the
'Red Pirates.' Now I'm asking you, Mary, wasn't that a
grand show? Don't I wish Miss Jenkins would drift in
too, and she's up to it. Why she'd just take one step and be
down the aisle leapin'; and if she was skatin'—you know,
coke, I mean, and they sells it in this burg by the bowl-
ful. . . . O Miss Collins, don't you want some powder for
yer nose too? They sell it for ten marks a deck here; serve
it by the barrel if you give them the sign."

The next ten minutes were spent by the two in remi-
niscing about chorus days in the "Red Pirates." "My god
Mary, I'd bead my eyelashes out six inches, and one night
—yuh remember—we all came out done up stinkin' with
pretty pink cheeks, supposed to look like honest to gawd
rough pirates you know, and the director took one look
at us and sez, 'For christ's sake, yer supposed to be men,
not bitches, when yer on the stage at least. Tomorrow
night you come out with real make-ups on or we'll im-
port a new load of fairies to take your places. This show
ain't to be used for cruising your trade while you're on
the stage at least.'" Miss Knight babbled on, and after
a breath continued, "and in the dressing room after the
show you couldn't see a one of us for the powder in the
air. We spent more time makin' up to go out on the street
cruisin' than we did in makin' up for the show. I'm tellin'
you, Mary, you shud 'a' seen us when we stepped out of
the stage door. Miss Jenkins got picked up by a cop one

day—in plain clothes—and he told her if she was caught out again with that calcimine make-up he'd put her in the jug. . . . But, my god Mary, these Berlin cops is different. Please, Mister officer, won't you arrest me? . . . I'm tellin' you, Mary, if I sticks around Berlin much longer they'll take me home in a little wooden box."

Miss Knight was so built that she could have passed as a real man; even her voice didn't generally give her away. It was not bass, but it functioned in the lower registers. She swore that she had passed herself off as rough trade upon occasions, but her instincts were all womanly and house-wifely. She liked to cook and sew, and she liked men, real men.

The life of Miss Knight had started some thirty years before in a little Illinois village, but her career proper had started when, at about seventeen, she went into a roadshow chorus. She didn't visit home often after that, though her family moved to Chicago two years after she left them. Speaking of one of her rare visits home she related:

"I hadn't seen the old woman for five years, so I sez to myself I'd drop in on her some afternoon, because I wuz playing that summer in a show in Chicago. I'd just had my hair hennaed and it was shinin' goldbrick. I wuz just sittin' myself easy in the parlor talkin' to my mother and sister when in comes my brother. Him and me never did like each other. He just took one look at me and walked out and a little later as I wuz going out he stopped me in the hall and sez, 'For christ's sake, yer a disgrace to the family.' I'm tellin' you, Mary, I didn't stick around home much. My brother ain't queer. He used to follow me when I went out cruising down State Street, and one night he wuz watching me from the other side and saw me pick up a soldier. That night when I went to visit the old lady just as I came into the house—bang!—he socked me just once on the jaw. I'm tellin' you, Mary, I snuk out of that house and didn't say nothing, not at all."

How long Miss Knight had sniffed cocaine she herself could not have said, because she didn't remember dates or think ideas, only the idea of the emotion at the moment. For ten years perhaps. At least she said her nose was paralyzed by now. "One night in Madrid—me an' my lover wuz puttin' on a show there—and I'm tellin' you I had some grand wardrobe then—gowns with beads all over them and gowns with silver and gold strings, with earrings that would knock you cold—I woke up one night shivering all over. I'm tellin' you, I thought I wuz going home in a crate the next day and I just grabs the pitcher of water from the washstand and drank six gallons right down at a gulp," he related one day, while recalling a dream of the night before that had nearly knocked him cold with despairing fright.

Miss Knight's chief complex was against elegance. The one thing she could not stand was to have some stuck-up bitch she'd known in the chorus get to acting elegant. For all her conversation about laying them out stinkin' when they got upstage, however, she actually drew into herself, or went away to unbosom herself with hurt to some more sympathetic being. Often she would herself in a moment of decision and ambition declare: "I'm tellin' you, Mary, I'm going to be elegant myself for a spell. Been as common as horseshit all my life, I have."

Miss Knight drifted into a Berlin café one night, looking to strangers much like a heavy-set, be-barbered travelling salesman from Holland or America. Soon she was at a table with other Americans, one only of whom had known her before, and it was from this one that she wished to learn where some of these queer cafés that she'd heard were all over Berlin were located. She informed the party that she'd just come from Italy, where she had been doing a female impersonation act. Before that she had been in Paris, where she had performed other acts, it could be surmised. Miss Knight felt a trifle ill at ease in the party she was with as none of the strangers were recognizable types to her. In her perplexity she was afraid that some of the members were upstage and elegant, and she couldn't judge whether they were queer or not, so that she could lay them out cold. A cautious reserve was forced upon her, and that was uncomfortable to so relaxed a disposition as hers. However, during the course of the conversation it was revealed to her that all of the party were quite aware of her biologic type, and were also ready to laugh at her rough comedy, without disapproving of her presence. Still her reserve kept her from revealing too much of herself by talkativeness. She listened. The conversation was a manufactured one; a bored one. Apparently before Miss Knight's entrance a discussion on European against American culture had been going on. One young man stated, with pompous pedantry, that "A cultured man is one who enjoys to the fullest all of his appetites and senses."

Another man, irritated by the atmosphere, evidently, responded curtly: "You're talking plain balls, Foster," culture is nothing but a matter of perception, plain intelligence, ability to observe things and conditions for what they are. Then maybe the senses can judge."

As Miss Knight listened and became aware that she need not feel ill at ease with these people, she also became uncomfortable at having the conversation so beyond her depths. So when the man who had first spoken said with an injured, over-refined air, as of one whose finer sensibilities are revolted: "Well, really, Jerome, we could have a gentlemanly discussion. . . ." Miss Knight felt called upon to relieve the situation. So she spoke:

"Now listen here, Mary—excuse me, just my way of talkin' you know—but are youse guys trying to get elegant? Don't do it, I'm askin' you. I'm common as dirt myself. Lay off this elegant stuff. An' Mizz Astor, won't you have another cup of tea—having a lovely time, so distinguished. Just grand, Mizz Astor. So glad you ast me over. What's yer name? Send me a postcard. I had a lovely time," Miss Knight chattered, having had four cognacs, so that her first caution and reserve were gone, as they easily did go in so impulsive a nature.

After these words Miss Knight went skating to the lavatory, and a few minutes later leapt back, with her eyes more concentrated into black pupils. "I'm snowbound now, Mary," she confided to inform the others that she had just sniffed cocaine. "Just coked to the eyeballs, you know, an' I'm lookin' for a bigger skatin' rink." Seating herself, she leaned back her head with a gesture meant to express hauteur, narrowed her eyes into a squint, and began at once to camp an imitation of "Miss Gwendolyn Rollins," who had been in the chorus with her, who had been with the Shuberts for twenty years without losing a spangle off her dress, and who had used to declare that when she played "Romeo and Juliet" there wasn't a dry seat in the house.

Though Miss Knight talked largely of an engagement she was to have at the Winter Garden, several weeks passed with no sign of her appearance. The night after the one which she had said she was to appear, she was still about, doing what the night-life and her finances permitted her. She was black with gloom except at moments when she was completely done up with cocaine; and she was completely without money so that unless someone invited her to drink she had not that release. However, she was not altogether unhappy because a number of Americans were about who laughed at her jokes, bought her drinks, lent her money, and liked her professional gaiety as a relief from after-war Berlin atmosphere. Some of them experimented with her cocaine, and always when there was a party or a collection of them her presence was permitted as a relief from pretentious intellectuality, personal antagonisms, and the morbid personalities of escaped Americans who were trying to make nihilism a cover for their ineffectuality. It seldom happened that some collection of Americans, or English, had not gathered by nine o'clock, somewhere, any night. However, some of the people who were ready to encounter her in cafés which they had visited "to see Berlin night-life" said it was a bore to have her greet them so familiarly in more respectable gathering places: the Adlon Hotel lobby, or semi-fashionable dance rendezvous.

Thanksgiving Day approached, and for days before Miss Knight talked of the magnificent dinner she would cook for everybody she knew in Berlin. She had a bare but large apartment which she had rented upon first arriving, and had paid three months in advance for while she still had money. Nostalgia, sentimentality about a real Thanksgiving dinner, and a wish to have some real American cooking, swelled her guest list to some twenty people, all of whom contributed money with which she might purchase a turkey, champagne, and other essentials for a real feed. Several of the guests assured her they would bring bottles of liquor with them.

After two days' preparation on Miss Knight's part, Thanksgiving Day came around, and her dinner party was scheduled for eight o'clock. As all her guests were aware of her eccentricity, she laid aside her men's clothing for the evening, and arrayed herself in a glittering garment made by herself. Upon her head she wore a bright red wig, and about her head she fastened an imitation but entirely gorgeous aigrette. Two German guests arrived. Miss Knight spoke German but poorly, and hardly knew how to entertain these first arrivals, and also she was in a fever about her dinner party. All the guests were at the moment a half-hour late. She felt tragic. At nine to nine-thirty other guests began to arrive, all of them semi- or completely intoxicated, in black moods, and fightingly antagonistic towards some other of the guests.

Kate Matthews came in, demanding immediately, "jes' one more cocktail to set me up, you know, Charlie, jes' one cognac to set . . . uh hic . . . to set me up." With Kate came Anne Simpson, a lumberjack-looking lesbian. Anne's latest love—an elaborately double-lived person— had left the day before to meet the man she was to marry in Paris, and in consequence, Anne had taken six decks of cocaine and uncounted cognacs—which she declared was the only safe drink to take when breathing snow. Foster Morris came in soddenly drunk, bringing with him a new soldier lover that he had picked up on the street in the afternoon. He was violently despondent and reckless because he had just discovered that a blond German boy he'd been keeping, and who had left him two days before, had taken with him Foster's evening suit, his diamond cuff links, and watch that was an old family heirloom. At a low moment he mumbled, however, soft with a readiness to forgive anybody anything, "perhaps he needed them worse than I do, though."

Miss Knight began to serve the dinner, and what other guests he had invited came in gradually, till there were eighteen in the party. With housewifely pride he brought in a great roasted turkey to display to his besotted and gloomy guests between whom only counter-currents of irritation were running. In displaying the platter he spilled gravy on his glittering gown. Foster Morris, who had been drinking steadily since his arrival, insisted upon carving and serving the turkey, and Miss Knight, who knew the grief of having lost a lover, permitted it. Turkey flesh, legs, and wings splattered about the room, to be rescued by the other guests and eaten. The lovely mashed potatoes, ornamentally placed upon a borrowed giltedged platter, went clattering to the floor from the hands of Kate Simpson. At ten-thirty the German man and wife departed, because, they explained later, though they did conduct a café for queer men they did not like seeing Foster Morris being unduly familiar with his soldier lover in front of them.

Soon after, the other guests departed, a good deal drunker than when they had come and still morose, though drunkenness had robbed their antagonisms of violence. The next day or so some of them explained to Miss Knight that it had been a wonderful party, but that something had just happened to get them all in the wrong mood. Miss Knight felt crushed for a time, but took more cocaine and on the third day, having discovered a beautiful blond policeman who was real rough trade, so he said, was quite convalesced. He would sit with his right hand in the left pocket of his policeman when they were in queer cafés, and would babble, "My god, Mary, I've got my hand on a real piece of meat at last, O Mary." He was additionally happy because Kate Matthews assured him that she, who could spot a queer man a mile off, knew that the policeman was just a war-made queer one, because he had tried to hold her hand.

One night there was to be a grand ball, and the word passed around that all queer people could go the limit with costumes and there would be no police interference. Miss Knight arrived as Madame Récamier, supposedly, but the neck of her gown was much less in evidence than in the well-known Madame Récamier portrait, for Miss Knight's bulky shoulders showed like the white flesh of a newly bathed coalheaver above all the glitter of her gown. Later she was elated with vanity and delight because of getting the first prize for costume display; until yet later she noticed that her policeman lover was getting amorous with Kate Matthews. It was Foster Morris who called her attention to the fact.

"My god, Kate thinks she's had a real man fall for her at last, and even if she doesn't want to break up your family she's excited, and she's so drunk she'll be careless. She hadn't ought to do it," Foster told Miss Knight.

Miss Knight was all wrought up. She went out into the hallway to take a sniff of coke behind the door. She was stricken with grief, anger, and desolation. Everything was turning bad on her. No money; no luck with her lovers; no friends, only people who thought she was a clown, but didn't want her around at decent places with them. After another breath of snow, however, she became understanding. She wasn't afraid really that Kate would attract her policeman. But she didn't trust Foster. Going back into

the main ballroom, she encountered Foster again, and remarked forgivingly of her policeman: "After all, though,
what they want is a woman, you know. They're real men.
They ain't queer bitches like you and me." Her voice
sounded like that of a mother of the world understanding
all things.

Within ten minutes, however, Kate's momentary hap-
piness was broken in upon by her superstition. She knew
things couldn't really happen well to her. She was sure
that she had seen two plain clothes men watching her in
the offing. It was her intuition, she declared, that let her
smell a raid a mile off, and she wasn't going to be arrested
in Berlin with her passport in the shape it was in. Kate,
a harmless soul, driven to drink and dope for company,
expression, and to escape eternal depression, seemed to
invite arrest. Already she'd been arrested in most of the
world's great cities—New York, Chicago, London, and
once already in Berlin. A born defect in her gait made
her look suspicious. Always she had been released and
apologized to, but she was getting leery, and was particularly so this night, when she was drunk, and at no one
could say what kind of a ball. Miss Knight, too, joined
in Kate's warning. "I'm tellin' yuh, Mary, I've been in so
many raids that I get a hunch of one a month ahead, and
I sez to all of you, and you can tell them elegant bitches
that try to pretend they ain't to me—Mizz Astor an' Mizz
Vanderbilt I mean—that I'm drifting right now."

A half hour later a party of Americans were installed
at a secluded midnight place that earlier in the evening
was too frightfully vicious to enter. They had dubbed it
Murder Cave because from four in the afternoon till ten
at night its *habitués* were all degradedly vicious types; off
the streets, complete dope fiends; down and out whores

grown too aged for street trade; cocaine merchants; and altogether cut-throat-looking types. By ten, however, the *patron* cleared most of these types out, or they themselves departed on errands surely not innocent.

At this hour, past twelve o'clock midnight, the place was supposed to be closed, but the *patron* of the place let the party in when he saw who they were. They were the only people in the place then, and the *patron* assured them that they could stay and drink as late as they wished. The atmosphere was confined and secretive. Most of the party spoke in whispers until Miss Knight, again happy as her policeman sat next her, began to converse in monologue, as though eternally playing to an audience:

"Did'ja ever hear of the Portland, Oregon Scandal? I wuz in it. I wuz at the Y.M.C.A.—in drag you know— some outfit I had too, stars and spangles and jewels all over me, Mary. Whoops my dear, you must come over, ah come on, come over an' call on me some afternoon. I never have nuthin' on afternoons. Just a lovely time you know. I'd just come from the theatre—had shown my act there you know, and then the cops came in and pinched us, and them Y.M.C.A. boys was scared stiff. They let me go because one of the plain clothes guys had seen my act at the theatre and I sez to him that I didn't know nuthin' about what kind of party it wuz, and had come there as a paid entertainer."

"But Mary, did I ever tell about the time in Rockyford, New York. I'd been to a drag dance with earrings on and wuz at the theatre when a man came up to me and held out his hand. He had my earrings which I hadn't noticed I lost. He sez: 'Are these yours?' and I sez, 'Yes,' and he sez: 'You'd better come with me to the police station.' My god, Mary, I wuz knocked cold, but I sez to him kinda nervous like: 'Wait a minute. You ain't in a hurry, are you?' I gotta get my wardrobe into a trunk because we got to go on to another town to show our show tomorrow.' He waited for me and after I collected what little sense I got I ast him if they wasn't some way we could fix it up, and he sez I'd have to call up the chief, so I did, and talked real refined and elegant over the phone. I'm tellin' you Mary, I can act like a real lady when I needs to, but that night I talked like rough trade—real manly tones— and I sez to the chief that I was sorry all this had happened and that it wouldn't happen again, and I had to be out of town tonight to play the next night with the show, and we wuz only stagin' a little act, and the chief talked it over with me for a while and finally sez, 'All right, but the next time *Mi*ster Knight'—and god Mary, you should of heard him dwell on that Mizz—'the next time you'd better not drop your earrings around so conspicuous.' My god Mary, when I wuz out of that I breathed better than coke's ever made me.

"And another time Miss Brachman—you know Miss Brachman, Carmen the second, sure you know her, a real grand bitch she is—you know her sure, that one that pencils her eyebrows so fine and uses a calcimine make-up— she was giving a real swell party at her apartment and all the rich bitches were there—a canvas out before her place like for a wedding or a funeral—and limousines and all sorts of private cars—and you shud a seen some of the drag costumes them bitches wore—cost five thousand dollars a costume some of them did, and honest to god jewelry. Well, the party was jest gettin' real gay when along comes a knock on the door and Miss Brachman shrieked out, 'the dicks,' and lifted up her skirts and ran down a sidestairs weepin', and I ran around like blind and finally got into the bathroom and back of the bath tub, and there wuz one of them real ladylike bitches and she kept on sayin': 'O if I'm caught I'll take poison; I can't stand the scandal,' and I sez to her, 'Close up, do you want to call in them dicks on us,' and she whimpered and shut her gab, and I sneaked out and locked the door, and when someone knocked, 'who's in there?' I heard a voice saying, 'that's the bathroom, and no one's in there,' and I don't know why, but the dicks didn't say the door had to be opened. O Mary, I'm tellin' you I've been in some raids, and you bet on a bitch's hunch, me and Kate both smelled a raid back there tonight. I bet that place back there now is being taken away in wagonloads of bitches in little black wagons."

Though Miss Knight's days in Berlin had not been joyful ones, it was just after this period that she began really to taste misery. Her repertoire of humor was exhausted so that people avoided her, and, themselves weary of Berlin, departed, or came no more to the places where they had been accustomed to assemble. Miss Knight found it difficult to locate people from whom she could borrow money to go on living.

At one of her darkest moments she had one flickering gleam of gleeful hope. Seated one night in a queer café she noted the entrance of a party of English swells: three men in evening clothes with two women, actresses or demimondaines. A few minutes later after their entrance a note was handed to Miss Knight from a man in the party. A few minutes later she was babbling about it.

"My god Mary, he's fallen for me at sight," she exclaimed excitedly, "an' Mizz Foster tells me he's a real Austrian duke. I'll be riding in a limousine next, with a grand elegant apartment all my own, next thing you know. Won't I be the upstage bitch then!"

Two nights later, however, Miss Knight was more than usually disconsolate and afraid that nobody liked her. She asked one man if they were all off her. "I'm a common piece of tird, but I ain't never pretended I wasn't. Whatcha all got against me just now because I'm hard up?" she queried, and a few minutes later, after being assured that she was not being turned against, confided: "My god, these Berlin bitches! Do you know that Austrian duke guy—well, I kept the appointment he asked for in his note and he went to my room with me, and he sez to me just as I was slipping pretty into my gorgeous lavender kimono, 'before we go any further I want you to understand that this will cost you a good sum of money. You Americans have plenty,' and I gasped and caught my breath, and got it quick, and I sez to him, 'Lookie here, Annie, you aristocratic bitch, just you put on your coat and run right along. Now run along, Annie.' I'm sayin' right now I ain't paying to sleep with no man. I get paid myself if there's any paying done. But I ain't having no luck at all these days. Losing my figure, I guess, or gettin' old, or those German bitches are too thick around, and they can live on nothin'." Miss Knight looked around her with a secretive air, lowered her voice a little, and confided on. "I suppose you'll be shocked and hold it against me if I tell you something—"

Upon being assured that nothing she could reveal would shock her listener, Miss Knight went on:

"You know just before I came to Berlin, and I was lined with money them days, you remember. Well, what do you think? You know I got stranded in Paris, and a guy

took me to a house where there were only men, and you
know, right away the Madame running the place offered
me a job, and I was hard up, and I stuck in that place for
months. . . . Now you are shocked, aren't you? Ain't I
always told you I wuz nothin' . . . . But Paris wasn't nothing like I'm gettin' it in Berlin, and I couldn't even get a
job in a house here. And do you know, last night I picked
up a cop. How that guy had the nerve to go home with
anybody I don't get. You know I hate—well, you know—
blind meat—you know what I mean." Miss Knight chattered, sure of the queer erudition of whoever happened
to be her listener, however bewildered and curious his or
her expression might be.

Having spontaneously confided all of his life that occurred to his mind at the moment, Miss Knight, recklessly
feeling the need for uplift, glided out to the water-closet
to take a deck of cocaine. Within three minutes she glided
back in the room, and out of a now gayer mood, and of an
habitual bitchy gaiety, shouted across the aisle to a German boy she knew, "O you Suzie Stoopantakit, I got your
number. It's—96—ain't it? You know dearie, I think yer
queer. Honest to god." Then, with a condor-like twist of
her neck and head, with eyes narrowed to "look 'em over
haughty-like," he declared to the whole room, "Whoops,
I'm so glad I'm a real man."

Such were the depressing circumstances of Miss
Knight's life at the moment, however, that gaiety did
not linger long, and he relapsed into moody confidences.
"O Mary, did I tell you about the dream I had last night?
I wuz paralyzed from my nose to the top of my head with
coke. Kinda blue, you maybe noticed I wuz last night, so
I took more'n usual. And I thought I wuz in a raid and

couldn't move, and then I woke up and drank six buck-
etsful of water like I always do, and I shivered inside and
out. I'm tellin' you I'll be taken out of Berlin all done up
like a mummy and stiff, if I ain't floating down the river.
And there ain't goin' to be nobody to send me flowers
either."

Again Miss Knight arose to retire. "I'm going to fly my
tin hip out just to powder my nose a little . . . who's that
yer looking at, Mr. Policeman?—No, sir, yer wrong, I
ain't queer. I'm a real man. What'd you say yer name wuz?
Send me a postcard. I had a lovely time."

Two days later Miss Knight had disappeared, black with
gloom. She had been reproached by Foster Morris for
having said that he was a coke fiend. Miss Knight denied
having remarked this, but was later confronted by the person she had made the remark to. Looking utterly beaten,
Miss Knight went out the back door of the café and was
not seen again by any of the people he knew in Berlin.
Those used to seeing him about, and knowing that he had
not a cent of money to get out of Berlin with, wondered
as to his whereabouts. It was generally concluded that he
was "floating down the river," into which despondency
and pennilessness had caused him to throw himself. Kate
Matthews, however, believed otherwise.

"No, sir, believe me, you can trust the bitches to take
care of themselves. He's probably alive and eating better
than any of us by now. Luck changes quick for them."

Six weeks passed, and Miss Knight had been well-nigh
forgotten, and when mentioned was only laughed at as
one of the world's exaggerated types, until one day Kate
Matthews was showing about a letter which she had re-
ceived from New York. It read:

Dear Kate,—Well, old dear, how are you? I
am back in U.S.A. How are all the others? Will
be back in Paris February 1st, 1922. I am sending you twenty-five dollars for the marks you
laid out for me, and hope that you will always
be my friend, as I love you and hope that you
are well.—I am, yours,

Charlie Knight.

"How in the devil did he get back to New York and
send back a letter to you in six weeks?" Foster Morris
marvelled. "He had not one sou on him when he went
out the back door because I called him down."

"Didn't I tell you the bitches could look out for themselves?" Kate Matthews responded. That one! If she was
run over by a truck or a steam roller she'd turn up, about
to appear in Paris or London or Madrid or Singapore.
She's just that international."

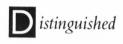istinguished

ir

Foster Graham stopped me that morning to say greetings and it struck me that he looked more rested, or less used, than he had a month back, when I last saw him. He explained by saying that he'd been in the country for two weeks. "That's the longest rest period I can stand now. Vacations are real work for me," he said, and his remark gave me a sense of how the ever narrowing circle of his activities was closing in upon him as he pursued excitement, continually more recklessly indifferent, and always more jaded in his nonchalance.

There was brilliance in the sky above the Tiergarten this autumn day in Berlin, and brilliance in the orange and red coloring against the coldness of the sky. Naturally, I felt alert, with a tingle of extra vitality through my limbs. So, swinging along carelessly, I had not been watchful about encountering anybody. Had I thought, I would have known that a presence would be irksome to me at this moment of high feeling.

Foster had been but two weeks before this in Paris, and he was pleased with the new wardrobe he had bought there, careful this time to see that every garment had a *chichi* touch. The trousers he wore were drawn in at the waist, and pleated there. The coat was padded smoothly at the shoulders, so that the descending line to the waist gave his figure a too obvious hourglass appearance. We had not spoken fifteen sentences to each other before Foster was camping, hands on hips, with a quick eye to notice every man who passed by.

"You're apt to get picked up in a way you don't want, and jugged," I suggested to him, cheerfully, as conversation, for I was sure that he had gone in for the sort of thing he did go in for, long enough to know how to take care of himself.

"Tut, tut, this isn't New York. It's a shame for me to make an effort to get off with anybody here, because they're all on their heels to start things themselves," Foster informed me, and then also told me that he'd just been at the coiffeur's, where he'd had his black hair waved. "I had them pluck my eyebrows too," he said airily, and twirled his waxed mustache. "I wouldn't look like this in Paris, but it goes down all right here." As he talked he looked so completely a fashion journal figurette that his camping manner, copied from stage fairies in America, sat strangely upon him.

Neither of us was at ease, because beyond the first minute there was nothing for us to say to each other. It was only that we were both Americans in a foreign city that made us speak. I scarcely knew how to avoid his dinner invitation, but decided to plead blatantly another engagement, and let him suspect it as nothing but a social lie.

"You're going to cut me, too, like old Timmons is, I take it," Foster said then. "I suppose I'm getting too much for any of you purposeful beings. Tut, tut, how will I stand your New England disapproval. We are so moral."

That was too much for me. After all of the yowl and yammer throughout America, amongst the groping intelligentsia, about the prudishness of the puritans, my Western soul rebelled. I could not be deemed New England. "Rot, Foster," I explained, "we'll have dinner together tomorrow night if you wish. I can't ask you to come with me to the house I'm dining at tonight, because I know the people too slightly. About Timmons, you're wrong. He's scolding all the time about everybody, but he can't disapprove of you violently, with his habits. It's only that you are difficult when you camp around people who don't understand. The manner is a damned cheap and flippant one anyway, if you ask me," I concluded.

"Don't tell me what he thinks," Foster told me. "He does that well for himself. The other day he informed me that he would speak to me, but that that was as far as he could go, since I was too married to the pissoir. But my god, dearie, one must have a tea engagement now and then."

"Yes, that. He also commented the other day on the way Ruth drank too freely—her copulating with whatever bottle she can get hold of, he called it—but you are certainly used to his irritations and aversions, aren't you? One does get fed up on too much of any one aspect of existence."

Foster, having started existence with some kind of sensibility, whatever had happened to it by this time, laughed nervously, as he attempted to be less facetious. "I know I'm a bore. But I can't go back to America, and I knew five years back I couldn't paint. What in hell? This is Berlin. . . . I suppose you've been working a good deal. . . ."

"Not too much," I answered Foster, as I wondered what he might do with his existence that made him like it better. "I'm just heading for Der Sturm, to see what new has been hung in the exhibition rooms there. Do you want to come along? Some of the paintings are apt to be as frenzied as you are, and it'll pass away an hour."

"Goodness me, Marjorie, I just love art. I love art," Foster minced, unable to be direct for over a moment. "Will there be some pretty pictures of naked boys? I just love art. It's too exquisite. So glad you asked me along."

He did not come, however, to my relief, and I did not

urge him. Not five minutes after I had left him I encountered Carrol Timmons, who was admiring a perfumery
bottle display with a great air of connoisseurship. The aspect of his elderly aunt-like visage did not particularly
please me, as I wanted the morning to myself, and was
in no mood to be amused by his deliberate gaiety, or his
continual halts to survey things in shop windows, but he
was going in the same direction as I was so we fell into
step. When I informed him that I had seen Foster, he said:

"O yes, Foster. Tiresome boy. I'm so glad it is you I ran
into. When you first spoke I was afraid it might be some
of the awful rats who have come to Berlin because of the
low exchange. Just too tiresome most of them are. I just
feel as if I would have to give up seeing people altogether.
And with this after-war atmosphere, and poverty amongst
the few really likable Germans one knows. It's all too
tragic, I suppose, but I just can't feel any further about
that sort of thing. People will starve to death; people
will die; or kill themselves, or drink themselves to death.
Now Foster has, or had, an air—real distinction—but life
has become just too much one thing for him. It's more
than enough having one's friends, let alone acquaintances
whom one accepts only because of worldliness, forever
thrusting their awful and limited realities in one's face.
Foster can be a nice thing, when he isn't drunk or in love,
or both, but such times are too rare. And when there are
such lovely window displays to see in the shops I can't
be bothered by people who bore me. But I suppose the
natives can't buy. How they must hate us foreigners. Of
course they know me—from before the war." Carrol con-
versed on, from irritation to complacency, back to irritation, and all the while his grey gaze appeared to be trying
to pry into the world's secrecies.

Agreeing that Foster could be less tiresome, I excused him, saying, "Of course he doesn't at all matter, not even to himself. He simply has to exhaust time as he can produce nothing, and he's probably despondent at his very inability to keep himself amused."

Carrol snorted. "My god, yes. I understand his futility, and might be sorry for him in a way if he only kept some distinction as a personal presence. But one can't go on forever being decent to him, and Ruth, with their worn-out, useless ideas. Always taking, taking, taking. Never giving anything. They just must live out their degenerate cycles. I don't see Ruth now, and when she dares come into a café where I am, I hardly look at her. I told her I was through with her, and you know me. She asks me repeatedly to come to tea, in the hope, I think, of having me back, but I tried twice and she was so stinking drunk both times with the cheapest kind of degenerates about her— lizards, cats, whatever they were, not men anyway. . . . Foster seems to feel it very keenly that I've stopped with him, too," Carrol talked on, saying the last with a satisfied air. It crossed my mind to be rudely frank for a moment and suggest to Carrol that he wasn't one of the world's givers, either, but instead I answered him:

"Poor old Ruth. It isn't her fault. There never was a way out for her, crippled up as she is. I remember in one of her enlightened moments she designated herself as a sentimentalist with the soul of a drunkard. With her at least it's just a terror of being alone. She must be batty in her belfry, and I know she has hallucinations that may come from d.t.'s, or might be just craziness. I'd just as soon miss viewing both her and Foster, Ruth particularly, when she is theosophical, or mystical." Within a minute or so after saying this I escaped from Carrol, saying I had an engagement elsewhere, and when free, discreetly forbore going to Der Sturm galleries, or to the American Express, where Ruth might be calling for her mail. The clear day had probably brought them all out. Now away from anyone I knew, and from the various pent-up and frustrated qualities they made me too keenly aware of in their presence, I felt exhilarated, liking the assurance of physical well-being which the crisp air gave me.

I was successful about having the day to myself until five o'clock in the afternoon, when in a glowing mood I drifted into the Hotel Adlon, after having lunched with an entire bottle of golden moselle wine, capped with café and two liqueurs. I'd decided I might as well have a cocktail or two, have dinner, more wine, and then take what the night offered me in the way of diversion: a show; a dance-hall visit; or a cabaret, perhaps. No sooner had I entered the Adlon than a voice spoke my name enthusiastically, and I turned to see Rudge Kepler, a cartoonist, who was in Berlin seeing what he could pick up from *Simplicissimus*. After leaving London, he informed me, he'd picked up with a pretty English girl who was travelling with him now. His great hulk swayed as he flung his arms about, and gesticulated with his hands in a large attempt to express his delight at seeing me. His greetings were always hearty, inclusive, and said as to an auditorium.

"Well, well, old timer. This is luck. Me and Goldie here were just looking for somebody to take us sight seeing, and I'll bet you know all the fast places to go to. Meet my friend, Goldie. This boy always knows all the swell places. He smells them out. Let's order some drinks while we talk things over," Kepler boomed on, gustily. I was glad to see him, though aware that his excess of loose vitality and enthusiasm was wearing at times; but my mood was not a critical one. He was full of plans to get out new folios, to start new comic magazines, to take a trip around the world meeting "great men" and "getting to the bottom of things." Goldie, the young lady with him, simply had no opportunity to explain how bored she was with existence; and Kepler had no ability whatever to understand boredom. It was to him a contemptible thing, a sign of weak bodies and weak minds; it did not have in it the quality of gusto, and virility, and strength, that caused him to make great swooping gestures in the air attempting to explain his admiration for whatever new "great men" he'd discovered; Dutch or Flemish masters generally. When I informed him that Carrol Timmons was in town he exclaimed breezily: "Ain't that fine? Good old Carrol. The last time I saw him he'd just bought a new overcoat, and ties, and cigarette cases. He was just that grand, man dear"—Kepler leaped into mimicry—"there are so many beautiful young things in the world"—and Kepler halted, for a moment wondering if he should be flippant—"but good old Carrol, we won't talk about his little eccentricities, will we? You know the last time I saw him he didn't seem any the less bitter at moments than always, in spite of Europe. A friend of his told me the doctors said there was nothing the matter with him. That he was simply a hypochondriac and suffered from a lack of vitality. But then you know old Carrol, and I'll bet he's hating Berlin like he always did New York."

Naturally I had dinner with Goldie and Kepler, and of course it was a good dinner with plenty of wine, because the re-meeting, the drink, and the sense of a needed fling-over after two months of quiet living, made me a person of great gestures too. There were cocktails; *pâté de foie,* three bottles of wine, pheasant, Russian eggs, pastry, coffee, and afterwards several *fines* to round out the meal. By the time this was finished it was nine-thirty. In our mood, of course, we had to step out and see a little life. As there was only Goldie for feminine companionship and as she did not care for dancing and as none of us liked champagne, we voted against the gold-digging dance places, and decided to look over the queer cafés. At any rate by now, with Kepler and Goldie, and illuminated with wine and liquor, I was bravely ready to encounter Carrol, Foster, Ruth, or anybody else that Berlin night-life had to offer. Kepler was eager too to have a look at what under-world life in Berlin could show him. I was only afraid that it wouldn't come up to his expectations for wildness, though it wasn't probable we'd stay sober enough to notice much anyway. Inside of half an hour we were seated at the Germania Palast, which was rather a show hangout, for men mainly. We felt sure that people some one of the three of us knew would drift in: from England, France, Scandinavia, Italy, or America.

Rudge Kepler was disposed to be resentful when we first struck the Palast; not because he had a combative nature, but because having drunk a little more than he carried all-consciously, he believed he needed to resent approaches to keep his dignity; for no sooner had we entered the long narrow café and progressed to a table at the back of the room, than shrieks, yodels, and cat-calls began to greet our ears. Some of them may have been aimed at our party.

"Whoops, dearie, I see you," sounded a falsetto voice, faking feminine tones. "Sisters Adlon are with us." The speaker, I noticed, was a man who had dined at a table near ours when we were at the Hotel Adlon. His manner at this moment was much different from what it had been then, when he was accompanied by two respectable-looking elderly ladies. As he shrieked out the barman noticed him, and immediately sent a pile of tin plates crashing to the floor, while laughter and cries came from all over the room. Within a minute the man from the Adlon was at the bar, ordering champagne to be served to all who would drink it. "I'll show these boys that us Americans aren't tight with money," he said with exhibitionistic generosity.

A few minutes later, as I had thought likely, Foster Graham came into the café, and passed our table to say good evening. He informed us that the man from the Adlon was a person from San Francisco, who had been involved in a grave scandal there, and who now lived on the continent in as abandoned a manner as possible. "He has three automobiles, and all the bitches in Berlin try to keep in with him. He's as much of a nut as they make them," Foster informed us.

After introducing Foster to Kepler, I suggested that we'd better get out, unless Kepler wanted to quiet down and take the place for what it was. Foster told Kepler too: "You have to take things as they come if you want to stay, because this place is protected by the police. The chief of police in Berlin is as queer as they make them himself. Anyway you needn't worry, they recognize that you're the B.M. stuff and just want to get a rise out of you. Don't be unkind to the poor things." So, warned to take all that happened humorously, Kepler became expansively good-natured and joked the various fairies about the room. He then ordered several rounds of drinks at our table, and began soon to relate a variety of fairy stories which he had heard while in the army, or about the sailors' training camp at Pelham Bay, New York, during the war.

While we were there an elderly fairy, well known to various psychoanalysts in Germany, came into the place. This night he was dressed as a blond-haired doll, and his fat old body looked in its doll's dress much like that of a barnstorming burlesque soubrette grown a generation or so too old for the part she played. All about the room at various tables were scattered the queer types of Berlin, many of them painted up, two or three in women's clothes, and a great number of types who were not obvious; who might have been mere sightseers, except that Foster generally knew them by sight and swore they were male whores.

Kepler consented after his fourth cognac to dance with Foster, as his heavy Germanic sense of humor had awakened to the ridiculousness of the scene. His great frame swayed about in the narrow space as he sprawled his arms and legs about in an octopus manner, unsure as to how drunk he actually was, or should properly appear. Other dancers on the floor, all men—there were only three real women in the place, one of them Goldie—could not abstain from kittenishly poking Kepler in the back as he danced around, but by the time he whirled to see who had poked him that person would have danced down the center of the room, while somebody else tickled him from the other side. As drink, however, had made Kepler recklessly good-natured, he only grunted mild objections, and after the dance seated himself, totteringly, but with a gesture of largely accepting all things in existence.

"Well, well, old kid, so this is the way they do it in Berlin. What. I mean to say . . . *Herrrrrrrrrrrrrr o-o-berrrrrrr, noch ein cognac, aber nein, noch vier cognac.* We can drink them, I guess, you old rounder." Kepler commanded drinks effusively.

Goldie, finding herself so out of it, decided to go back to the hotel, and she didn't want Kepler to miss his night, particularly as he was drunk and she was sure he'd be obstreperous if she made him go with her now. Once in a taxi, she said, she'd be all right. It took me about three minutes to see her on her way, and when I came back into the café it was to find that in so short a time Kepler had fallen off into an intoxicated doze. I decided to let him sleep for a quarter of an hour, as he would surely insist upon ordering more drinks if he were awakened, and my stomach was not up to them. It was in fact in such a condition that I decided to play Roman banqueteer.

For the first time in months, so he said, and just by coincidence on this night when Kepler and I had come, Carrol Timmons came into the Palast. "This place is too erotically upsetting for me, as a steady diet," he informed me, as he gazed with a tolerantly critical eye all about him. Noting his cheerful mood I wondered if he had no companion with him. Though I did not discover who the companion was at the moment, in this man- and smoke-filled room, Carrol informed me:

"Such a nice boy, too; just the type that attracts me most. Such a gentle face, and so rich physically. I was quite upset about him last week, because he came home with me one night, and the experience was wonderful —wonderful. . . ." Carrol rolled his fiercely spinsterly eyes expressively, "but he disappeared the next day and I thought I had been taken in by another whore. But I understand now. Of course he is German, and has no money, and has to do things he doesn't want for money. Must support his mother, you know. One of those tragic cases; a well-established family before the war. And I had no extra money to spare him. I told him pretty frankly what I thought of him when he didn't show up the second day, but as long as he came back. . . . Well perhaps he does care for me a little for myself, you know. It's so comforting to think that anyway."

"Oh the devil, Carrol," I said crossly, still sick in my stomach from too much mixed drink, "why try to make romantic affairs out of these ten-mark-bought bitches? Why in hell should they care for you, for yourself alone? If you're remarkable for anything it's for a kind of brain you have at some moments, and not at these kinds of moments, I should judge."

Carrol, to my surprise, was not offended. "I know, I know," he confessed, "so foolish of me, and how often I have been disillusioned, but after New England, and that absurd moral bugaboo pursuing me for so many years, and then the snap, and the feeling of release within myself . . . but there's Foster at my table. I'll have to go back to my boy, I see. Foster doesn't seem to understand a thing about playing the game fairly."

Foster came back to our table, laughing flippantly, and said, "Dearie, the Countess has a new lover, and she's green-eyed if I go near her Marjorie." He was staggeringly drunk, and insisted upon dancing again with Kepler, but Kepler did not awake easily, and so was let to snore on. Finally he came torpidly to life when Ruth came into the café and joined our table with much loving acclaim. She had not been there a minute before a German boy came to the table and took her aside, to sell her cocaine, I learned later. As neither Kepler nor I had ever tried it, we decided to invest in a deck each, so as to keep awake if we were to go on through the night. Ruth was holding forth, being the social lady.

"You old dear, how glad I am to see you," she burbled

to me, as she sat as erect as her intoxicated state let her. "I just keep a little stock of this powder on hand, you know, for when I get blue. Of course I don't overdo it. How I do love seeing you again, you old dear. Why don't you ever look me up? I never see you anymore. You must come up and have lunch, and then—you know what lunch means—always the best wines at my place, and plenty to drink—of course you'll stay to tea, and dinner—and afterwards we could vary the program and get into our swell rags and go dancing in an elegant manner. Tomorrow, say. I won't be sentimental, or tell you my troubles. Timmons, the cranky old bear—I wouldn't be as bitter with other people as he is for the world—has scolded me enough about that."

"Some day, surely, Ruth," I assured her.

"And we can just have one long talk about old times, New York, and all the people that we used to be around together with."

"You're getting your dates mixed in fond reminiscence," I told her. "We never knew each other in New York and I know darn few of the hangouts there. I'm a farmer boy myself."

"Why, that is so. It's only here we met. I always forget, you dear old thing. You know, you look so much like Jim, my husband that was, though he is yet, even if he does live with another woman."

I laughed uncomfortably, having at other times heard Ruth tell several other men, quite unlike me, that they looked exactly like Jim. Foster whispered in my ear: "Look out, Ruth's wanting some other companion than a bottle tonight, I guess. Whenever she pulls that 'you remind me of my husband' line, veer away, that's my advice."

"What is a poor woman to do in this world," Ruth mourned, "and even for me—and you know how broad-minded I am—Foster is becoming impossible. I'm as kind-hearted as they make them, and I always say—now that I know more of the world—that people's habits about certain things are only a matter of geography, but I do wish Foster wouldn't act as he does with his lovers in front of me. See him dancing there now," as Foster danced by, drunkenly falling over the man he was dancing with. Ruth was holding her third whiskey and soda in her hand, and tried with wabbling dignity to sit straight. She held a jewelled walking stick in the other hand and attempted to get some support from it. Pausing for several moments while her fuzzy mind performed a few slow volutions and seemed to stop at the idea that she had better assert her purely detached and scientific interest in all of this, she collected herself to say:

"Never in all the times I have come here have I ever been treated as anything but a lady. I'm a Gale-Cawkins, and I do know how to assert my dignity if it is necessary, but a lady does not need to advertise the fact," she assured me, and twitched her head "to look the lady" before she relapsed into blinking at space. She came out of this semi-coma only now and then to murmur sentimentally:

"You dear thing. You will come and see me, won't you? There are so few Americans about, and you do look so much like my husband."

"Hell, let's get out of here," I jerked out suddenly to Kepler as a sudden coagulation of aversions occurred within me, and bad temper robbed me of any ability to laugh. I'd noticed Foster getting increasingly maudlin with a soldier, and Carrol Timmons, down the room, was being sloppily affectionate with the boy at his side.

"It's a devil of a lot better to know some people for what they can think, or for how they appear on the street, than for how they act in these near bedroom scenes," I reflected, as Kepler and I went down the aisle.

"You're leaving, are you?" Timmons asked me.

"Yep, that's it, Carrol," I answered. "I'm not up to watching this long unless I'm drunk, and I'm not, having just thrown up. And Foster is apt to be losing his lover, or wanting to borrow money. Ruth's teariness is enough without his being added."

"Yes, yes, poor Foster. He must have something to adore, or worship. His is an essentially religious nature, as he told me one day in regretting that he'd lost the faith of his boyhood. I'd like remaining friends with him, but one just can't, you understand, of course."

"Too well, Carrol. It's bad if you let yourself get caught up when you see the spectacle it is."

"I assuredly shan't mess up things."

"Oh I know. Fair enough of course, and there's no such thing as messing up one's life. It's not that I mean. Any kind of expression is cleaner than pent-up repression, and it's not so apt to reproduce itself in other generations. But it is the wanting of emotion, by the pretense of it. You'd better be commercial in this atmosphere I would judge, rather than sentimental. If you can stand the atmosphere as more than an exhibit of what people can become."

"Good Christ, yes," Carrol said, angry at some too-realized experience of life within him. "I get so tired of the demands of my physical nature. These boys are all right, the most they can be for what they've had a chance to know, but, my god, they must have difficulty in knowing which are their own bodies, and which limbs are their own, after all the gymnastics and promiscuity they've been through. I must admit that my nostrils and my mental will rebel against my own carnal desires, but one can't be so cowardly as never to seek release."

"Nothing to be added, I guess. We all do what we do and will do, so it might as well be flagrant, I suppose," I muttered, as my mind had struck a complete snag.

Out on the street the racy quality of the night autumnal air freed my laden senses from the oppression of limited and sordid realities. Kepler too awoke more to vitality, and began to talk of seeing more of Berlin night-life. Feeling somewhat tired, and potentially sleepy, I was, however, ready to make a night of it, but suggested that if we were to go on we'd better take a sniff of the cocaine we had to liven us up. Getting under an archway entrance, away from the wind, and under the light of a near street lamp, we unfolded the paper containing the cocaine, and cautiously sniffed a little. Feeling no immediate sensation, to be aware whether we'd actually taken any into our nostrils or not, or had blown it away, we sniffed a second time. My nose began soon to feel numbed, and in the back of my throat there was a dryness that was mildly disagreeable, while a feeling of nausea was within my stomach. However I felt exhilarated, strong, leapingly light-bodied, and capable of going on without thought of tiredness. Kepler was affected in a similar manner, so we started off at a great pace towards a big dance hall, where I knew there would be plenty of girls to dance with. "They won't insist upon your buying them unless you want to," I told Kepler, "and if you slip them fifty cents' worth of marks that will seem a fortune to them."

The Palais de Danse was so full of people that it was impossible to get a table, but we did not mind, as that meant we need not order champagne, and could drink what we wished at the bar. There were several Americans in the bar-room; college or prep-school boys, or sailors in civies, and some of them became friendly in the slap-you-on-the-back American manner immediately, glad to see anybody from "home."

"Hell, I sez to the waiter," one noisy prep-school boy was soon explaining, "I've got money. What d'you want? I'll pay. Give me the best table in the place. When he wouldn't even give me a table I asked to see the proprietor, and showed him my card as soon as I saw him, and what d'you think? He owns a shoe store that stocks stuff from my dad's wholesale house in America. I showed him I had more'n four hundred dollars on me. You can damn well bet I got the best table there was going. Come on boys, now all together, let's have another drink. On me, this one, fellows, all of you. And we'll have to give them some college yells."

Swaggering on thus, he finally took a great roll of marks out of his pocket. Everybody around the bar was quite ready to drink on him, as we were too, aware that he'd be bled elsewhere if not here. He noticed a plump, buxom, blonde girl, in a floppy peach-red hat, standing nearby, and reached out to pull her hat.

"*Was denn?*" she said, haughtily offended.

"That's all right, kid," the prep-school boy exclaimed. "Some one who speaks Dutch tell her that it's all right. I just wanted to offer her a drink. Here—see this—fifty thousand marks—take this—an' come on, kiddo. Get chummy."

The blonde lady, eyeing the money, slowly relaxed her dignity, but she did not yet release a smile. She was evidently wondering whether she should take the money, or wait, on the chance that she could get more out of this young *Auslander*. However, there the money was in her face. So she took it, as though joking, and stuck it in her stocking. The boy was a little taken aback, but did not know how to ask for his money after all his grand display. So he danced with her.

It was past two o'clock before this dance place closed, and we stayed until the end, dancing or drinking most of the time. Kepler had picked up a girl who looked sensible to both of us, and who spoke English. She was quietly dressed, and seemed to have no gold-digging desires. "Get 'em old and be nice to 'em," Kepler advised me. "She'll take us around sightseeing tonight, she says, and see that we don't get done in."

Getting a taxi, the three of us went off to a *Nachtlokal* in the Kurfurstendam section of the city. The place was concealed behind trees in the midst of a plot of ground surrounded by a high iron rail fence. A long winding pathway led up to the entrance of the house, which seemed dark until one got inside. Here there was a fair-sized dance floor, with a not bad American jazz band playing, so we sat at a table and ordered champagne. I got up to dance with a luxuriantly flashy lady who informed me she was Spanish, and asked if she could sit at our table. I waited, however, until I was back at our table and took the word of the lady with us that we'd better not ask the Spaniard to join our party. "She makes trouble," our guest informed me.

"*Was sagen sie?*" the Spanish girl hurled at our friend, whereupon a word battle waged that I feared was going to come to a hair-pulling contest, or to blows, but it finally calmed down, and we were told by the girl with us that the other was always coked up and violently combative. I was more careful about asking girls to dance with me, till, standing over by the piano, after having asked the orchestra to play "Blue Danube Blues," a girl took my arm and asked me to dance with her. I had noticed her, and her party, made up of another girl, and an Englishman, all three of whom were well dressed, and looked a good sort.

The girl who asked me to dance with her spoke English fairly well, but was morose at the moment, as regards conversation. "Let me take fifty marks," she asked me, and I did so, thinking she might be very hard up, as she seemed not to be an ordinary cocotte. Her clothes were evidently expensive and well made; they consisted of a black velvet suit with the skirt trimmed with gray fur, and flaring out at the bottom; a chic hat resembling an Egyptian head-piece, made of purple velvet with a gold design worked into it. I liked her appearance much: her tall, well-formed body, and her face, with a prominent nose, intelligent eyes, and a generous, full-lipped mouth. When I came over to ask her to dance with me a little later, the man at the table turned on me viciously, so that I feared he was going to raise the devil because I'd butted in. However, his complaint was that I'd given the girl— Flora—money for cocaine. I assured him that I had not known she wanted the money for that.

"Hell yes," he answered, "what else would she want it for in a place like this? Now that she's off again she'll be off for a couple of weeks. She isn't a prostitute. It goes against her. I know what this cocaine business is."

As he spoke I got a smell of his breath, like that of stale blood and onions mixed, and realized that he, and then probably too the other girl with him, were cocaine addicts. As Flora was dancing with somebody else I asked him if he minded my dancing with the girl with him.

"Not at all. Do by all means. She likes dancing, and I'm

no good at it, am I, darling?" he said, and added, "and I'll have a glass brought so you can have a drink with us," which I was ready to do as Kepler seemed contented to dance every dance with the girl he'd brought along.

The second girl I danced with was decidedly beautiful, and recklessly indifferent of the fact, which she must have known. The loose-fitting, pale green dress that clung to her slender body, was very low at the neck, and one side of it fell away from her shoulder continually, showing the brilliant white texture of her neck and bosom flesh. Her eyes had a brightness and a beauty given them by cocaine expansion, and her pale features were quite perfect. She could scarcely stand to dance because of drink, or cocaine, or both. Once we had started dancing, however, when I held her up, she felt the music and danced freely and well.

"Don't mind what Jack says," she told me. "He gets all wrought up and nervous sometimes. Thinks he has to pretend that he's not down and out, and is trying to save me. He was an officer in the colonies and doesn't want to have to go back to army life, and there's nothing else he can do. But he doesn't need to save me. I'm not wanting that. I have a good time. Two months, a year, finished, and that's as it should be." As she talked, in spite of her remarks, I felt that she was cheerful, and had little morbidity within her. She continued:

"I like dancing and a good time. Even if there hadn't been the war, things must be boring when one gets old. What's the use of being serious about it all as Jack is. One only lives once, but that's enough. It isn't as though this country weren't all smashed to pieces either. I'm half English, but my nationality is German, and I couldn't get on in England, so Jack stays here with me. He won't marry me though, but that doesn't matter."

By four o'clock, when Flora said she was tired of this place and wanted to go elsewhere, Kepler and I were ready too. The Englishman and his girl stayed on at the place, while we four others located a taxi after a little search, and were driven to an address Flora knew, on the outskirts of the city.

"I don't know what this place is like, but you have to take what comes at this hour in the morning," Flora informed us. "I want to stay up and go to the O-la-la at six when it opens, to get something to eat." Flora said little else. She was not unfriendly in her manner, but had a decidedly morbid temperament, and seemed, as Jack had hinted, to be just recovering from a love affair in which the man had deserted her. Arriving at a house on a terraced hill, we went through an iron gate, and were soon inside the house, three rooms of which were lighted, and set with small tables. An elderly woman pounded out pieces of dance music at intervals, wearily mechanical. A few world-worn-looking people were strewn about the room, at tables, drinking champagne without undue gaiety. We seated ourselves and gave the order. So we sat, attempting now and then to dance when the music thrummed, or attempting conversation in a listless manner when it was not sounding. Thus an hour and three-quarters passed in a drowsy manner, as we were all either sleepy or feeling low.

During this time three solo dancers came out to perform; all of them completely nude, and no one of them able to dance even a belly dance well. There was no reason, in fact, for their performances, as their bodies were not well made, and no one in the place was apt to be interested or startled by nudity. Flora expressed her boredom morosely, or moped, and it was she who suggested that we leave, get a taxi, and go on where we could have something to eat. The O-la-la, she told me, was an after-night place into which all night-lifers in Berlin drifted, as a round-up of their pastimes. En route there, however, Flora stopped the taxi at another little café, saying that it was easier to procure cocaine there than at the O-la-la. Kepler and I remonstrated with her a little, though she paid no attention to us, but simply took the attitude that her habits had been formed before she ran into us last night, and that her life and habits would go on after today, when we would probably never see each other again. As her will was strong, and her mood not one to brook interference if we had had interfering dispositions, she had her way.

This café was little more than a small room, but there were nearly twenty people here, mainly men, seated at tables along the sides of the room, and some who stood in front of or to the side of the bar. Entering, we seated ourselves at once in front of the bar, and ordered black coffee with *fine,* to waken us a trifle. A rather dowdy, dark-skinned girl began to talk to me immediately, while some of the men got into conversation with Kepler, who spoke German better than I. These regular *habitués* were interested in us because we were foreigners and perhaps wealthy. The girl talking to me informed me in broken English that she was a Russian refugee, and had once been with the Russian Ballet. She took a silver box out of her bag and offered me cocaine on a tiny silver spoon which was an accessory to the box. She was rather grudging about giving any to Flora, so I took the spoon, breathed lightly on it, and passed it on to Flora, fearing that otherwise there would be a quarrel between the two girls. An old, wispish man sat at the piano drumming out music;

so as there was a narrow space between the tables along the aisle, the Russian girl and I began to dance, together at first, then alone, interpretively, moving empty chairs out of the way as our dance became more violent. I began to feel much livelier, having had another *fine*. Our dance was apparently an unusual sign of life to the *habitués* of this café, and it amused them, so they were amiable about moving themselves out of the way. When the piano player stopped playing I talked to him, insisting that he was a very fine musician, and that it was too bad he didn't have a better place in which to present his talents.

"*Ja, aber man muss vor den geld spielen,*" he informed me, in a melancholy but confiding manner, seeming to recognize in me an understanding soul. I did my best to converse about music with him, in my hash-German, and as a result he was soon playing "classical" music—Sibelius, Moussorgsky, Rimsky-Korsakov, Grieg. As the Russian girl wanted to go on dancing, and as Flora, having now purchased some cocaine of a sharp-faced, red-haired German, was content to stay here for a time, we dismissed the taxi, and remained, while the Russian girl and I danced continually, music or no music. I felt lightheaded, but afraid I should be nauseatedly sick in my stomach if I didn't keep moving. The only interruption to our dancing was when we stopped for a few moments to gulp down a glass of cognac; then we went back immediately at our dancing, which became more interpretive, solemn, and laden with dolorous significances, as time passed. While the musician was playing a heavily tragic piece, I, feeling headachey, took to dancing with my head bending towards the floor, and my arms dragging as near the floor as possible while retaining a foothold; this went on probably for about ten minutes, until I realized that my dance partner was drink-

ing at the bar, so I too desisted, and joined the others.
Leaving the bar for a minute to stand against the wall
until the blood would cease rushing vertiginously to my
head, I stood beside the piano where the sharp-faced German cocaine dealer tried to get into a conversation with
me. Another young man, of whom I had no intoxicated
distrust as I had for the German, also talked to me, informing me that he was Polish, and did not like this place,
but only came here because it was warm. I noticed too
that two middle-aged men were talking to Kepler, and
that the girl who was with him was keeping a discreet eye
on all of us to see that we were not imposed upon. We
were all of us, but her, dazed-mindedly drifting along,
and not apt to offer much resistance to whatever might
happen. When the cocaine dealer tried to get affectionate
with me, and kissed me on the cheek, I pushed him away
with feeble protest. The Polish boy took my arm, warn-
ingly, informing me, what I was ready to believe, that the
German was *schlecht* (bad). He also became affectionate, as
the men around Kepler were attempting to become with
him, and Kepler's protest was no more violent than mine
had been. I felt vaguely resentful towards Flora, who, it
seemed, could have paid more attention to me than she
did, but it was easy to be seen that she was interested in
her own morbidity at the time.

By eight o'clock the pangs of hunger drove us again
towards the O-la-la, and as we went the cocaine dealer,
the Polish boy, and two men with Kepler, accompanied
us, and we permitted their presence nonchalantly, real-
izing that we had no right to refuse their wish to go to
the O-la-la, or wherever they wanted to go. Anyway the
present place was closing, and it was cold out, so that they
probably only wanted to go somewhere to keep warm,

and I felt confident that they would not manage to rob us of anything with Kepler's girl watching. Two taxis were necessary, and we soon arrived at the O-la-la, which had a small bar-room with a larger dining and dance room, to the side. Taking a table we each ordered what food we wished, and some of us went on dancing, for a piano was being played here also, by a member of the jazz orchestra from the place where we had accumulated Flora.

There were a good number of people here already, and during our stay many others came in, most of the people who arrived being better dressed than I had expected. One blonde lady, who was a musical comedy actress, and charming to look at, was much in evidence because a night out had added to her natural vivacity. Flora could not be kept from the bar, not because she wished to drink, but because, apparently, she liked sitting on a high stool and leaning despondently upon her elbow. She got into a conversation with a matronly looking woman of some forty years. When I approached her she was not communicative, so I talked to the older woman, who spoke English with but a slight accent.

"She's blue today, poor girl. I've been telling her she has got hold of something nice—you—but she just says that she can't expect enough money to mean anything to her. She says she was used to spending a thousand marks a night herself before the war, when a mark meant something. I try to tell her she might as well be sensible and accept the change, but she's blue today. I guess the man she was living with has gone away with somebody else," this woman explained to me, and later seemed to suggest that if Flora wouldn't be amiable there were others that would be. She also told me that she herself had used to be with the Opera in Munich, and offered to give me notes to singers she knew there, if I intended visiting Munich; and she gave me the addresses of several bohemian hangouts in that city.

It was no surprise to me when Ruth and Foster showed up, and in high spirits, in spite of the fact that Foster's blond soldier had left him last night, making, however, a sleeping appointment for another night, three days later. Ruth had been to her apartment since I'd seen her last night, and had, indiscreetly I thought, put on a valuable sable coat which she declared gave her *chic*.

"You know, you dear thing, I may not be a beauty, but I do have *chic*," Ruth informed me. "I know how to select and wear hats, and my wardrobe—well, I am presentable wherever I go, and you may not believe it, but men do try to get off with me, though naturally I soon let them know by my manner that I'm not that kind of a woman. Of course I look rich, and they may want money—but even in the Adlon a very well dressed man—but there I go. I will be vain. You dear thing. When are you coming to lunch with me," Ruth held forth, feeling, as always, expansive. She insisted upon buying drinks for everybody she knew; she was, in fact, ready to buy drinks for everybody who came up and talked to her, anxious as she was always to keep people about her. "Money, what is it, with this exchange?" she philosophized, "I've always been a good fellow, haven't I, Foster, and even if some people will gossip just because a woman—I am a Gale-Cawkins after all—happens to be broad-minded."

There was a great commotion at the door, and a wild-eyed woman appeared, staggering between two men who wanted her not to come here to judge by their actions, but their desires in the matter meant nothing to her, and she was vehemently expressing her intentions of doing well what she wanted. It took no second glance to recognize that she was "coked to the eye-balls," and completely intoxicated besides. Her hair was flying loosely about her feverish, glistening-eyed face. Seating herself at the bar she lopped first to one side and then to the other, all the while indulging in sporadic conversation with herself, or with whoever spoke to her. There was justice in the comment of the musical comedy actress that she looked like Medusa on the rampage. However, Medusa-like as she might look, she had no intention of humbly subsiding, and when the actress, for some reason resentful of her, tried to take one of the two stools over which she lopped her large frame, there was an immediate row, and the actress was forced to retire, as it was quite evident that if the row came to a physical encounter she would be completely dishevelled, routed, and sent down to defeat.

I retired for some minutes to the water-closet to be sick, and there dimly heard a great commotion going on outside, but judged that it was only Flora, or the Medusa, or the actress, in some quarrel with each other, or with some of the men about. When I came back into the room, however, I found that the place had been raided by policemen, who claimed that this was a place where unregistered prostitutes congregated, and said that every woman must go to the police station with them. Flora, by claiming that she was here with her husband, and perhaps by giving one of the policemen money, had managed to be spared, as had the actress and the Medusa, who was a well known character to the police. The girl with Kepler, it proved, was the wife, or lady at least, of one of the American jazz band men, so she too was secure; but Ruth, in spite of being little more than a harmless dipsomaniac and religious sentimentalist, had been taken off bodily to the police station. She had not taken her American passport with her. Foster accompanied her through a misty rain that had started, and came back half an hour later to inform me that she was let off after some explanations.

"Trust poor old Ruth," Foster said, "she couldn't get off with a man if she paid him, but she would get taken in by every raiding party that comes along. She seems to invite arrests. I'm off going with her. She's a hoodoo. It's a sure bet there'll be a raid if she's around. And she's as moral, sexually, as they come."

"I didn't know you retained any concept of morality, Foster," I commented.

"I don't. I haven't even the conception of sex any longer. It's just 'how amusing a bed companion are you' with me."

"Ho, ho, ho, that's good," Kepler guffawed, coming out of a torpor over his last whiskey and soda, now that he had put three orders of ham and eggs into himself. "It ain't important, I guess. You just get rid of what's in you, and whatever else you are is something else besides." Drunk, Kepler lapsed into a Scandinavian English.

"It's all a damn bore except the few times when it isn't, if you ask me," I added. "This hand-me-down, quick order, bargain variety, wholesale, that one sees in Berlin certainly doesn't give sex an aspect of luxury."

We passed nearly three hours in this place, dancing, watching rows, singing snatches of vulgar or sentimental songs, and eating, so it appeared about time to be wending our way homewards, as it was nearly noon. I suggested this to Kepler, who, while distinctly drowsy, had moments of life now and then. Flora had not recovered from her morbidity and disgust, but she was more amiable than she had been earlier. The cocaine dealer, the Polish boy, and two other men, as well as Flora, and the

girl with Kepler, wanted to accompany us. I hesitated
for a moment, wondering if they did not just want to
know where we lived, but soon rejected that cautious idea
as too cautious. So we all started off, the first address
which we gave the taxi driver being the address of my
room, which lay in the Tiergarten neighborhood. Arriving there, I reflected that my room was an immense one,
with three great chairs, a lounge, a divan, and a huge bed
in it. As it was now noon, I decided that I would only
take a nap since I had a tea engagement at four o'clock,
so I told them all to come up to my room and sprawl
themselves about as best they could. I had a vague feeling that most of the people had no rooms to go to, or
that if they had, they were far away. They all accepted the
invitation, so we climbed up the two flights of stairs and
went into my room. Kepler, Flora, Kepler's girl, and I
sprawled ourselves in uncomfortable postures across the
huge bed, while the other men slumped into chairs, on
the lounge, or on the divan. Soon the sound of snores
began to vibrate through the room, and I too fell off into
a heavy sleep, in spite of a decision that I should only nap
for a few minutes.

It was after three o'clock in the afternoon before I awoke
with any real consciousness. My nap had been fitful,
and full of nightmares through which people, animals,
and strange objects had proceeded, in a series of grotesque, disconnected dramas. Awaking, I tried to collect
my senses, and it seemed to me that six days had passed
since the night before when I'd started out to show Kepler
and Goldie the sights of Berlin. I had a panicky smoth-
ered feeling of terror about life, and a nauseated belief that
I had broken two engagements, one to occur at tea that
afternoon, and another to occur two days later. It was

an astonishment to me when I saw all the people strewn about the room, and I at first could not recall how they had got there. Finally, however, I dimly, as through a heavy fog, recalled and remembered that I had locked the door of my room and had the key in my pocket. This precaution I had taken so that none of them could leave, taking any of my things with them.

I waked all of them but Kepler and the two girls, and gently insinuated that it was time for them to be off. The cocaine dealer was the only one disposed not to accept the hint, and became threatening, which angered me. The three other men appeared to dislike him, and took my side. I told him to get to hell out of the room damned quick, or there'd be trouble, and jerked Kepler awake, and the cocaine dealer subsided when he saw we had no fear of blackmail threats. Soon he and two men departed. The Polish boy lingered to explain that he suspected the cocaine dealer had taken money out of Kepler's coat. His suspicions were correct, or at least Kepler had a thousand marks less than he thought he should have.

Before the three men had departed I had given them each a part of five hundred marks; but the Polish boy had been reluctant to take any. Now, however, he said to me:

"You are a rich man. I used to be when I lived in Poland on my father's estate: not rich, but well off. The war. . . ."

"Yes, yes, I know," I broke in hastily. "Too bad, all of that. What can we say, though? No, I'm not rich. It's just the exchange. But you'd better take this," and he was persuaded to take five hundred marks, whereupon he left, he or the circumstances having managed to make me feel confused and mean, as though I were in a way responsible for the economic condition of these people in the midst of whom I'd dissipated. There was no use doubting any of their stories; true or not their tales of former wealth, they were evidently now poverty stricken, and surely did not eat often. Consulting my finances, I concluded that, in spite of the expenditures of the night before, I could, by being careful of my expenses for some weeks, manage to give Flora five thousand marks, so I woke her and the other girl and we were soon departed from the *pension*. Before we left, however, I hastily threw my clothes into two suitcases, as I intended spending two quiet weeks in Potsdam before going on to Italy.

After the girls had left us, Kepler and I agreed, on the tide of a hangover gloom, that we would have no more nights like this—at least until the next time. It was really too depressing to see so much of a kind of life that one had not consciously helped to cause, and could not do much to alter.

Arriving at the Adlon where I had a tea engagement with an elderly English woman, I waited for her to come in. While waiting, I saw Foster Graham across the room, and he came over to say hello. He looked even more the exquisite than he had yesterday, as he had on another new suit of soft grey texture that fitted his slight figure in too glove-like a manner. His socks were of iron grey silk; his shoes were the final thing in neatness and style; and he carried an obviously expensive cane. I wondered how he could continue, with the night-life he led, to look so nonchalantly poised and contained. As for myself, I felt, after one night, dragged out, and near the undertaker's hands. I wished Foster to go away and not talk to me, but he at once began to talk.

"That blond soldier of mine can go hang himself. You should see what I picked up along Unter den Linden this morning. A Russian boy I used to see in Paris, and who would never pay any attention to me there. But O boy, now. . . ."

"Lay off the chatter, Foster, for the love of Mike," I groaned. "If you can stand so much repetition and boredom, I can't."

"Are you having dinner with me tonight?" he asked.

"Hell, no. I'm headed for the country, Foster. It's no use. I'll have to be frank enough to say you'd bore me with your conversation, and I certainly would be a dead weight myself. Anyway, I can get myself into thick atmosphere sufficiently alone, without your trained aid."

"Another time then. . . ."

"That's too far ahead. I leave for the country tonight. I want to get out of Berlin. This is no place for a man of impressionable amiability, if the amiability could stand the strain."

Kepler passed through the lobby, having been upstairs shaving and cleaning up. Goldie was with him. She looked well groomed, but irate, and her glance at me was a cold one.

"Yes, we leave for Munich tonight," she informed me austerely. "I insist upon that. If Rudge thinks I will stay alone in this hotel while he wanders out again tonight with that awful woman, whoever she was, who led you around last night, he's mistaken. We go to Munich, or I go back to Paris."

I bid the three of them a hearty good-bye, as I saw the Englishwoman standing in the middle of the lobby looking for me, and had to join her for our tea engagement. As I walked across the floor I decided that she would have to do most of the talking, because if I began narrating, my line of conversation would surely bring forth a moral lecture from her.

"You look very fagged," she commented.

"O yes; too much pounding away at the typewriter, that's all. My nerves are rather jumpy. Do you mind if I have a whiskey and soda rather than tea?" I answered.

The

odging

ouse

The landlady came to the door. Tall, blonde, heavy set, phlegmatic, and while at first seemingly suspicious of auslanders, she gave in easily to Harold Files' arguments, and let him have the large back room for one-half the price she had first quoted. It was his nonchalance, he supposed, that won, and perhaps his first suspicion that she was a cocaine fiend was correct so that she was easy to sway. That would not matter, however. His passport was in order, and he felt sure that if the woman had the usual landlady's ability to judge characters she would already have assumed that imposing upon him would not be too easy a matter. The landlady smiled graciously as she turned to leave the room. He utilized charm upon her, knowing what a nuisance it is to have an unfriendly landlady.

In the room was sufficient space to entertain ten people if he so wished at any time. There was a huge, low-based bed; one large easy chair and several smaller ones; and shelf and wardrobe room for all varieties of clothes, books, wine and liquor bottles, paintings to be stored, and whatever litter was apt to accumulate.

He cleaned himself quickly and dressed to go out for dinner. Berlin was boring him; this needed move to have a decent room at a reasonable price annoyed him. Still the present room seemed satisfactory. At some vainer moment he'd be glad of the full length mirror in the room, but tonight his face irritated him, as did his slender, sloping body.

Wanting release from a fagged but smouldering impatience, Files went out and dined at a restaurant where an orchestra was playing mainly Viennese waltzes, or selections from the more romantic operas. From there, on the strength of an amiable glow put within him by a bottle of moselle wine, he went on to a dance cabaret. It was four o'clock when he ventured homewards, and before the door of the lodging house his attention was arrested by a scene two doors ahead. Two women, evidently much intoxicated, were arguing vehemently about being let in. A surly German assured them that they could not enter, and angrily inquired why they persisted in ringing the bell to awaken him. This was not their residence.

"Thizz—lem'me by er I'll ged by anyway," one of the women answered him, swaying her tall, mannishly slender body as she groped persistently at the door to force an entrance. It was evident that she did not understand the surly Prussian's torrent of German. "Thizz—eightsheven Nurnberg—str—asse," she hiccoughed.

Files watched for a minute, doubtfully, and somewhat resentful of the crabbed manner of the Prussian concierge. He was bored with the surliness that a certain type of Prussian possesses, and utilizes, particularly on auslanders, and on such foreigners perhaps as were allowing themselves to be charged three times the amount the law permitted for rooms. Simply because there had been a war was no cause for an ill-mannered ruffian such as that man to display his vile disposition to American women. Files, fairly intoxicated at this moment, was feeling combative and patriotic: quite enough so to stand up for the rights of misused womanhood as against Prussian militaristically trained tyranny of manner.

"What's the matter here?" he inquired in austere tones of the German concierge. The Prussian explained morosely that these two women, who were *schlecht,* had been ringing his doorbell for the last half hour, when he had already told them three times that this was not their address. He also declared that he had no love for women who were men. Files, upon looking closer at the two women recognized their type. Both of them had their hair cut like boys, and the larger of them was dressed like a man in every detail with the exception of a skirt. The other was not so exaggerated a specimen.

"Goddam German," the larger of the two girls muttered. "Shays he'll call the police. What's the use? The whole police force is queer. I'm gonna get in there and get to my room. What to hell is it to him what we are?"

"I guesh yer wrong, though," Files told the lady. "Thish isn't 87, you know. That's where I live, too, and it's two doors down the street."

Mollified, and confiding, the antagonistic spirited girl, who had been doing the arguing, turned to Files, saying: "Good, someone who speaks American. You tell him. He gives me an ache in my fanny. I say, lesh none of us go to bed yet. Come on, lesh go and have another drink somewheres. I know all the plaiches in Berlin."

Files, feeling in no way drowsy, was ready to accept the invitation, though intuition told him that the girl would be rough to deal with in her drunken state. However, a second thought assured him that she was not actually so difficult as she was exhibitionistic with her pugilistic mannerisms. So he agreed, and after a search the three people located a taxi and were off towards an address which the girl gave.

"Steve Rath is my name," this girl told him when they were in the taxi. "When I was in America, it was Stephanie, and I wasn't wise, but that isn't it. I'm no girl, but it took Berlin to teach me what the trouble with me was. I always knew something was wrong. This girl's Russian I guess. We don't savvy each other when we speak, but what's the use of people saying anything to each other anyway."

Upon arriving at the rendezvous address it looked for a moment as though Files at least was not going to be permitted to enter, but Steve brushed aside the objections of the man at the entrance: "Thash all right; a friend of mine, and you get to hell out of my way or I'll knock you for a goal," she assured that porter, and her assurance was sufficiently belligerent for him to move aside. Steve said further to Files, "S'too bad you don't look girlish, kiddo, sho's you could pass off as a girl in drag—men's clothes, you know—this joint's all for women."

Steve had no sooner murmured this remark than she was taken away by an onrush of women. It was evident to Files that she was the belle of the place, and that all of the other *habitués* desired her dance favors and her attention. She, however, was not feeling sociable; in fact, she confided upon sitting at the table which he had already selected that she was fed up with having these German bitches try to get off with her simply because she was a foreigner, and they thought she was wealthy.

"Damned whores, all of them. What'd they think? I'm no whore. I'm not promiscuous. Shay waiter, bring us three whiskies, and quick, get me."

The taxi drive had sobered Files somewhat, and the whiskey sobered him still more, aided as it was by his own alien feeling in this atmosphere. He had previously in the evening reached the saturation point, and was rounding into the cycle of devastating sobriety, a quickly reached sobriety that made his observations over-cruel to his own intelligence and emotions. How in hell had he let himself be dragged to a hole such as this? The room was full of mannish-looking, or at least mannishly groomed women, except that the word "groomed" could not be used on people who looked as the ones in this room did. They all appeared underfed, and their gaiety had not even a feverishness. It was apathetically mechanical. Steve, he noticed, however, seemed out of atmosphere too. She was magnificent to look at now, and if her blackish eyes had not given her away, the reckless manner in which she placed cocaine upon the side of her closed hand and sniffed it with an experienced gesture soon let him know that she was utterly irresponsible through an overdose of the drug.

"How many decks of that stuff have you taken tonight?" he asked her.

"I dunno, maybe a dozen," Steve assured him nonchalantly, and her tone was tinged with resentment. He knew she would readily tell him to go to the devil.

"It can't be that much, or you'd be a corpse, wouldn't you?" he inquired.

"Huh, not me. You can't kill me. Not that I care. But I drink cognac with it, and get drunk, and the effect's not so bad."

"Cognac and whiskey are bad things to mix then. Hadn't you better stick to the one drink?"

"To hell. What'd I care? Hey, waiter, bring me another cognac."

As Steve was dancing with the Russian girl, Files observed her. She was six feet tall, slender, and well formed. She could easily have passed off as an eighteen-year-old boy were she in boy's clothing. The shape and cut of her head was boyish too, and young leonine. It was easy to see that she was a child to this environment, for her swagger was too exaggerated, and in spite of oft-asserted violence she was easy to persuade so long as he did not use an authoritative tone upon her. Suddenly she broke away from the Russian girl and asserted: "I want Mabel. Where is she? No, don't argue with me. Who to hell are you? You're nothing to me. Where's Mabel?"

The porter at the door came into the room to aid in pacifying Steve, but she was not to be pacified. She pushed various waitresses and women away with great violence. Her tall frame swayed in the middle of the smelly, smoky room, like that of a mad young Samson searching for pillars to jerk down. Her short dishevelled hair, and her purplish eyes set in a chalk-white face, made her a spectacle to regard with awe. The Russian girl, nearly weeping, pleaded with her in German, which Steve did not understand, to come home, not to drink any more, and not, surely not, to take any more cocaine. But Steve persisted in her wild demand for Mabel, who was apparently not around anywhere. She was calmed down for a few minutes, however, and reseated herself, muttering that she must have Mabel: where was she? And at last, though Files had thought that Mabel might be somebody out of her past life, Mabel arrived and proved to be a very drab looking German girl. No sooner had she arrived than Steve's desire for her presence was gone, and Mabel's efforts to be affectionate met a vicious rebuff. "Keep your hands off me. I'm going on to another joint. I'm fed up with this hangout," Steve declared, and turned viciously, but vaguely, and in her turning caught sight of Files in the range of her vision. "This is a hell of a joint for a man. What the devil did I bring you here for? Come on, let's jes you and me go somewhere else," she asked of him.

The Russian girl, however, insisted upon remaining and followed the two out upon the street. Files, having decided that he was bored with Berlin night-life, wanted to go home but was reluctant to leave Steve alone, coked up as she was, and intent upon going to vice joints. He was aware though that if Steve was to be got home it meant a struggle, tact, apparent acquiescence to her will, and persistence. As he had never known her before, it struck him that the job wasn't his. However, he decided to see it through. So when a taxi had been procured, he countermanded an address she had given to the driver, and gave the address of their rooming house. Steve did not notice the direction as she had slumped into sullen gloom. When the taxi arrived at 87 Nurnbergerstrasse, however, Steve did notice, and refused to budge. Told that it was five-thirty, and that there was no place to go at this hour, she was not convinced and swore she knew her Berlin. Asked if she didn't know that any place now would be as boring as the one they'd left, if all of night-life isn't actually boring anyway, she responded that life is that, and that she was going on. When the Russian girl tried to woo her out of the taxi she became violent at once. At last, however, Files won with a suggestion that they all go up to his room and have just one drink out of a whiskey bottle he had before going on.

"It's the real hot stuff you know, Steve. Some I brought from Ireland—pre-war. You don't get anything like it in Berlin, or much of anywhere these days. Come along, and then we can think where we'll head for next. I know a joint that opens up at six, and it's only five-thirty now, and this place I know has more class than any of the others. It's the after-night place for all the swell dance places and for actors."

Once upstairs, and with a whiskey in her, Steve was not so insistent upon moving. The December air outside had been freezingly cold, though Steve in her drunkenness had not noticed it until she got into a warm room, and there, before the fireplace, she decided to stay. There was no suggesting to her that she go into her own room, as she said it was cold in there, and she didn't give a damn what that old coke fiend and brothel-housekeeper of a landlady would think if she were found in Files' room in the morning.

"The maid's caught me with things in my room and in situations that would have had me kicked out a week ago if the landlady was going to raise a row. The people in this neighborhood are used to anything. Half of Berlin is made up of bitches anyway," Steve argued, feebly now. Speech was not a strong point with her. She had also decided that she wanted to talk about life, or at least that she wanted to hear it talked about. The latter would be better, as she was not very articulate about what she felt, or thought she felt, and she declared she was tired of thinking.

The Russian girl, seeing Steve so adamant, and feeling out of place, left. Steve had only picked her up at a lesbian café anyway, Files was informed. So Steve sat looking sadly into the wood burning in the fireplace.

"I don't know what I want—do you?" she confided.

"I guess not," Files responded, "if anybody ever knows what he wants. It's taking what you get, or what you can make yourself think you want, I suppose. How do you happen to be in Berlin?"

"My father married another woman and I couldn't stand her, and I was restless in America, and in London, too, so I thought I'd take a chance on this. I liked it the first month because it was so wild, and anything could happen without questions. But I don't know. What to hell? I can't stand people. I guess I'd better coke and drink myself to death about as quick as possible. I don't like it anyway. Not any of it."

"Do you do anything?"

"I thought I was going to be a musician, or maybe a dancer, but I can't get a studio, or I can't get a piano, or I can't get anybody who can play music the way I want it to be played if I decide that it's a dancer I'm going to be. And now I have to go to Munich and get a girl I'm in love with. She's married, and I thought there was no chance because she didn't like women, but I've heard something that makes it different. She doesn't like her husband, and isn't with him, and she said she was attracted to me."

"You're choosing a rocky road if you're going in for professional love. Do you find it worth while?"

"I don't know. What to hell? Give me another whiskey will you. I wish I had something to read. What books are those on your mantel shelf?"

After about an hour's conversation with interims of silence longer than those of speech, Files laid himself upon the broad bed, and informed Steve she could do likewise if she wished. "We can nap like this, in our clothes, until we wake up, and then we will go and get something to eat," he told her. He soon fell off into a heavy sleep out of which he was awakened, in the midst of an unpleasant dream that seemed to have a realer presence within it than dreams generally have. Steve was embracing him blindly, as a crawling worm, her mouth pressed closely to his as she mumbled "Give it to me. Give it to me. Give me your tongue."

Files sat up after pushing her away. "What—what's this?" he muttered before he was wholly awakened, and then, rational, added, "O yes, you."

"It isn't me you want?" Steve mumbled, and Files saw

that she was completely intoxicated, and unaware of what she was doing, so he merely answered, "No, and it's not me you want. That's all right. Lie down and try to get a little sleep. I'll ring for some coffee and I'll wake you when it comes." As he arose and looked about the room he noted that the bottle of whiskey, which had been a quarter full when he had started his nap, was empty. Steve, once he had lifted her body straight upon the bed, and placed her head upon the pillow, fell to sleep. Files went out of the house and into a restaurant where he ordered eggs and coffee, which he ate after taking three aspirin tablets. Within a half hour he went back to his room. Steve was still sleeping, but it was by now twelve o'clock noon, so he rang the bell and when the maid came, told her to bring coffee to the room. When it arrived he awakened Steve so that she could drink it black, and thus somewhat sober herself.

"I've got to cut out nights like this. I've gotta get down to work, goddam it. I must—I must," Steve said, morosely, without convincing Files that she would do so. By now he recognized the undeveloped child quality she possessed; a lost dumbness and bewilderment of face and of attitude. He surmised that as long as he was at this rooming place she'd be around him a good deal simply because she was lonely, and disgust of the atmospheres in places such as she had been frequenting would cause her to seek different companionship at other than reckless moments. Well, it didn't matter. He could talk to her and try to buck up her spirits perhaps, and by now her type of being could not depress him, because her despondencies did not come much within the range of his own mood problems.

There was a knock at the door, and when the knocker

was told to enter, a heavy-set man near middle age came in, and was greeted with ironic humor by Steve.

"Hello, you old hellraiser," Steve said. How'd you find out I was here?"

"The maid told me."

"Meet my old friend, Files, and this fellow's a hard-boiled egg, too, Jerry Anderson—that's what he says his name is, anyway," Steve presented the stranger.

"I've had bad news, and I needed a talk with you to cheer me up," Anderson said to Steve. "You're so cheery a body with your spontaneous gaiety and girlishness."

"Christ, don't start camping at me this morning. I'm fed up," Steve said in surly good nature. "What's your trouble? You can talk about anything, I guess, in front of this fellow. At least he went to my hangouts with me last night without squealing. I was trying to lambaste my way into the wrong house and he picked me up."

Jerry Anderson was mottled red and yellow on his cauli-flower-like face. His ears were purplish red. When he smiled the remnant of what once might have been called charm by some people revealed itself, but Files felt uncomfortable because of the older man's too obvious auntie-like manner. He began to wonder if he had not better change his rooming house. Under his breath to Steve he spoke:

"Are all the roomers at this place queer women, or bug-gers and fairies?"

"Ho, Jerry, you should hear that," Steve said. "He got you at once," and then she answered Files: "There are two Englishmen that are lovers staying down the hall beyond the L, and there are two American girls that aren't any-thing, if you ask me, in the two rooms this way from them. But you can't ever tell what drifts into this house because the landlady takes in anything that comes along just so long as they pay her, so that she can have money to keep stocked with cocaine. But Jerry's better than he looks at first glance in the morning. None of us are pretty sights now, are we?"

"That boy of mine—the one I had in Venice—is bothering me again. He found my address somewhere, and has written me," Anderson said to Steve. "I'm afraid he'll try and join me here. His family would go to any ends to get him off their hands. That's what comes of taking a boy off the streets in Italy. They always try to blackmail you, but he ought to know I haven't any money. If he comes here I'm finished. I won't know how to kick him out, I'm that tender-hearted."

"Tell him to get to hell out the moment he arrives, or let me do it for you, Jerry. When a thing's over it's over, and the best thing is to cut it off quick, and as rough as is necessary," Steve said.

Steve, having had coffee after dabbling ice-cold water over her face, was becoming livelier, and now that she was confronted with somebody else's problem, her manner took on an almost officious efficiency. It was easy to note that she delighted in patronizing and advising her friend Jerry, for at no moment now did the baby-whimpering manner of lostness rest upon her.

"I'll fool him; I'll slip off to Greece, or at least to Constantinople, that's what I'll do," Anderson brooded. "And that boy of mine—my son I mean of course—has gone and got himself into a mess again, borrowing money from friends of mine, and telling them to ask me for the payment. He's put some gad of a girl in a family way too, after all the preventative training I've given him. And to think I broke him in myself when he was twelve years old—the safest way, with men, and that time with his own old man."

"You're blowing off wind now, Jerry," Steve answered him. "There isn't any use because I don't think you'll shock the audience you have, so dry up on that line. And come down to business. Have you any liquor in your room? I drank the whole bottle of whiskey in here last night, and with my hangover I have to go on drinking now."

"As a matter of fact, however," Files interrupted, "I have an engagement over town and have to be getting on, so let's all get outside and have a drink somewhere else. We'll encounter later, perhaps."

As the three were going out, Files noticed several pieces of luggage standing in the hallway.

It belonged to a young woman who was conversing with the landlady about the price of a room which she was to have. She was having trouble to understand or to make herself understood, so Files offered his assistance.

"Thank you so much. I have forgotten all of my German, as I haven't been in the country since I was twelve years old," the newcomer said to him after he had translated back and forth for her. "I wonder how I shall like Berlin after Monte Carlo. I have been hearing such tales of the brilliance of the life here. One gets so bored and restless, doesn't one? I feel as though I might stay here a long time—two weeks at least. Where does one go for amusement?" Her appearance was a distinguished one, and Files wondered how she had drifted into such a rooming house, for it could be seen by her luggage and dress that she was of the world that demands service. Immediately his own manner became professionally worldly.

"That's difficult to say, isn't it, unless you indicate what has been boring you last so that one can suggest a variation to you."

"If you only would. I should rest, somewhere in the country I suppose, but I'm not keyed to that just yet. Whatever does one do about so many things anyway?"

"We were just going out ourselves to take a parting cocktail, or *fine,* at whatever place we can locate near here. Won't you come along?" Files invited.

"Indeed I will. I need just that."

Steve, who had been talking and laughing easily with Anderson, became silent as she looked over the new young lady with potential suspicion. As she went out the door her body had a battling cock gesture. Her left shoulder was lifted higher than her right; she walked with a pugilistic swagger that seemed to say she would stand for no rough stuff being pulled on her without there being an immediate combat. However, over a cognac at a nearby bar-room she relaxed, and deigned to look admiringly at the outfit of the newcomer, who had introduced herself as Hilda Gay, a name which both Steve and Files knew of.

Miss Gay was vividly black-haired, pale, green-eyed, with cerise-colored lips, and a presence that was entirely metallic, and as efficiently ongoing as a well regulated machine. Certainly to the casual eye it appeared that what she wanted she would go out and get, and while Files could not actually know, it appeared to him that she had not even a curt interest in Steve or Anderson. Perhaps she had spotted him as her immediate game, for she directed all of her conversation at him. Hard-lined of body, thin, tall because of erectness, she had the shine of polished silver about her, and the electricity of magnetized steel. It came time for Files to depart, and he so stated, in bidding good-bye.

"Bless you for helping me, and for letting me know all three of you," Hilda said then. "I came to Berlin on an impulse, knowing nobody, as I've gone so many places before, but I haven't always been so fortunate at immediately encountering someone whom one feels one can talk to, and I do feel you such a person. We surely will see each other again, won't we? O yes, why ask that even? We must and shall." As she began to speak her voice had a trained softness of cooing machine wooing within it; for a sentence or so it had a quality of trained society narration; and its ending tones were those of surely gripping its prey with professional tenderness of implied amour. Her hand held that of Files in a firm grip that for the moment suggested easy fellowship of worldliness, but still left the question open for a more significant pressure. So Files left. Within him was a tingle, of alcohol, of possible adventure to come, of a curiosity repelled and at the same time fascinated. Well, whatever the game was he was game. Upon arriving downtown, however, he found that he was expected to spend the week-end at Potsdam with a friend, so there he went in spite of a feeling that he was breaking an unspoken-of rendezvous with Miss Gay. If she really knew nobody in Berlin, they might have danced together that night. However, she might still be in Berlin after two days, and if the bird had so quickly flown—well, well!

A day had passed since her arrival in Berlin, and Hilda Gay sat in her room, still in bed, attempting to read a French novel which was supposed at the moment to be "important." But she could not read. It was too bad the

young man she'd seen yesterday hadn't been around since
the drink they'd had together with two other people—so
awful both of them—at the bar. Why had people told her
Berlin was gay? Already she hated the place. And he had
been—what was a way to describe his quality if she had
wished to speak of him to anybody—yes, charm, foolish as the word was, that was the quickest way to say it.
He had charm. There was a something about the way his
head sat upon his neck, and a naïve quality too. She supposed this was to be another one of her leches. He must be
coming back. She would find out from the landlady what
his name was and leave a note, or if not from the landlady
even from that impossible lesbian that he had been with.
So she wrote:

> Dear (she would find out his name later).
> Do come in to see me. I'm in room number
> ten, and Berlin is being simply impossible for
> me. You will understand, and I'm sure you can
> tell me where the places to go are. (Should
> she write anything personal?—yes, after all he
> had been shy and once he answered she would
> know how to manage). I did so like you, you
> know. Just one of those quick intuitions of
> another person's quality that one gets. Surely
> we must know each other better. Do come.
> I'm simply locked in my room trying to forget
> time and space with books and letter writing.
> Yours,
>   *Hilda Gay.*

Having written the note she rang the bell and sent for
the landlady. Before that person had arrived she felt res-

tive, until she had the name "Files," and had given the note
to the maid to leave where he would surely get it. Whereupon she arose and got into a brocade dressing gown that
she was aware looked well upon her lithe body. What was
there to do?

How the shining, bright, wide, long room grew dull,
charcoal-textured grey, small, and confining, with smoth-
ering walls surrounding, against which her arrogant desires and resentments beat; then again how its walls fell
away so that the room was not there; so that vapors in the
mind struggled to have a realization, to think, to escape
the forever-hovering waking nightmare of frustrated carnal and other desires groping through her subconscious.
The room sank, was sinking, was not there, as everything
else that might possibly have a reality was not there. This
was nauseating, to the will. This devastated her pride.
Perhaps she was an ill person. Was there no calm or rest in
her? She must dress for the evening and go out for another
ghastly late night, on chance. Already the landlady had
told her that Files would not be back until the next day.
Why had she come here? Why was this not Monte Carlo
or Rome or Paris—anywhere where she knew people to
reach by telephone or taxi? She must even see if either of
those two other people were in. They might advise her
of places to go to for music, vibration, a living scene of
some kind. Berlin, for her, and why—after the war, to
come to a city so enveloped in after-war atmosphere? But
of course she had been driven by the madness of her boredom from Monte Carlo, where every morning after a so-
called gay party she had been suffocated with a detestation
of stupidities.

As she stood before the full-length mirror and curled
her black bobbed hair about her ears, Hilda felt that she

could not look at her face, at her body, not in any way to judge her appearance. Not tonight. She struck herself as too distorted. Hell, had people ever called that beauty. . . . Well, yes, after all, to be sensible for a moment rather than hysterical inside herself, yes, and indeed yes. One must keep that much for oneself. She herself had known herself to be electric with magnetism at times. Were her getting-off days past now? How had she struck that man Files— (how well she remembered the way he had walked as he had gone down the street)—

She put a silver and black band with a small orchid on the side of it about her head, and after having applied make-up to her eyes, cheeks, and lips, a sense of being able to make a picture of herself began to dwell within her again. She must exaggerate beyond the usual exaggeration of artificiality, and achieve a more shining glitter, a harder hardness.

The picture was being painted. A lust for conquest began to arise triumphantly within her so that she worked quickly and nervously. The blue and silver gown which flashed—brilliant blue in the broad pleats, that opened as she walked—competed and qualified with her own applied coloring. Now she was ready to go out, but where— perhaps, after all, that man Files might come back from Potsdam sooner than he had said. Surely that place would bore him. She knew that he wasn't the type to like the country—not Potsdam country. Now—well, she would write a letter or two while thinking of what to do. To Ivor Jenkins, perhaps—no, that was done with. He had just been a makeshift anyway between others who had been makeshifts between the one or two she had cared at all about.

As she sat at the writing table she was still thinking

about whom to write to, or where to go on the chance of encountering somebody that she might dance with. Would they let an unescorted woman into dance places in Berlin? Perhaps with her arrogance she could force them to. Then there could be champagne to put a sparkle of vitality in her, and there was no telling who might be about to dance with. She ended her note to Ben Greenwood, scribbling: "I'm longing to see you. We must and shall meet again, bless you. Love, Hilda."

Stamping it, she left the letter for the maid to post, and hurried out of the room, intending to go to the Hotel Adlon, there to discover dance places. She would go to one and say that she must enter to await the arrival of a Mr. Somebody or other. She intended that they should let her pass, and there would be no nonsense on the part of a dance café porter towards her in the mood that she was in now. One could at least demand things of restaurants and servants and cities if one couldn't put across one's demands on life.

A restless wild vitality ran through her. There must be some place to satisfy her need for moving life that she was a part of. So she walked quickly down the hall and down the stairs, till suddenly she stopped quickly, as if sharply pained. Was that he talking in the hallway?—Yes! . . . That was sharp reason for gratitude that stung her with relief. . . .

"Good evening, Mr. Files. I sent a note to your room about an hour ago," Hilda declared, coming up to Files. "This awful Berlin. You must help me. What does one do? I have dressed simply to pass the time away, and I intended to dine at the Adlon alone. You must come with me. You must not have another engagement. Both of you," Hilda said this last in desperation, putting into her helplessly hopeless-driven voice all of the helpless lady appeal which training had taught her was difficult for the listener to rebuff.

"Ah—er—well, yes. You know—that is—I'll be glad to go and have dinner somewhere with you," Files answered, not taken aback but ill at ease at her recklessly given invitation to both of them. Steve, he knew, would be difficult to deal with once she had drink in her. "Miss Rath has another invitation, I believe," he continued, ruthless about giving the hint to Steve that she had better not come along. After all, he argued to himself, he was sure that Miss Gay was not interested in women and Steve would surely start trying to get off with her as soon as she had one cocktail.

"O, I *am* so sorry," Hilda said, turning perfunctorily to Steve, and quickly returned in her remarks to Files. "You can come now. I have a taxi waiting."

Files followed out of the door.

"There really was no taxi waiting, of course, but I did sense that you were bored talking to that—girl, didn't I?" Hilda said, harsh insect-voiced, with a trickle of grasshopper laughter.

In a taxi a minute later Hilda sank back, calmed at least from the wildness of seeing an unaccompanied evening ahead of her. She regarded Files' profile, and the clearness of his neck. Tenderness caught her. She wished to hold him in her arms. "Bless you, you darling. I wonder if you've known how much I've thought of you after that small encounter. You were so immediately sympathetic to me," she informed him.

"That was nice. I thought of you too," Files answered, courteously. A tiredness and apathy was on him. He supposed he wasn't playing up as warmly as he should, and then he felt her hand under his chin, caressing it. "Kiss me," she said. He did. Hilda felt a lush feeling of desire gush up within her; she held her lips closer to his and leaned nearer to place her arms about him. "Yes, yes, it must be. I do want you," she said huskily, with yet a rasp of machinery in her voice. "You do understand?"

"I do. Some of us always want so many, and if we drink much tonight and go to dance I'm sure I'll be wanting about everybody in the room, until I really look closer, at the individual. Suppose you're the same."

Hilda moved back to her place in the taxi and was silent for a minute, and when she spoke, her dry, insect voice—voice of the insect horde—voice in despair against the wind—went on, again taking up its but slightly varied refrain: "What does one do in the face of so much of it? One can't forever go on saying that kind of thing, but I feel it. Indeed yes. One feels that kind of emotion—so often."

"And it gets one into—not messes or trouble, because anyone with pride in this generation can't recognize anything actually as a trouble or a mess so long as one keeps above water—but it does complicate existence. There's too much one does simply out of not knowing what to do: then standing the complications becomes damned tiresome."

Hilda felt coldness run through her. Was his remark meant for a rebuff?

"Indeed yes, that too," she murmured. "But we must dance this evening. What champagne can do for people who feel as we do, and particularly when we're both so free."

"It's strange you're in Berlin, after France," Files said, changing the conversation and curious about her.

"Yes—my mother. She would come to Monte Carlo

simply because I was there. She never will understand that my world is not hers. But how often I have felt that. There's nothing much one can say about that sort of thing, I can tell you," Hilda told him, a wail of sophistication in the voice; a thin waver and a rasp in her thin tired mechanical tone that varied at this moment only with the wail and a slight accent of exasperation, an exasperation at her realization that she wasn't really getting to Files. This wasn't sympathy. He would listen to her, but his interest was not actually involved. How one is deceived! He had seemed so easy of approach the other day, but now there was this barrier of tired worldliness that he was putting up between them. For a moment she believed she would let it go, but her eye took an evaluating glance of him, and again that lush feeling of desire swelled up within her. Her imagination took him as she would have him in a most intimate relationship. Neither her will nor her tenderness of carnality would let her believe she could accept defeat, and really she did not know that he held back. They must drink tonight. Some men are so stupidly awkward and unready quickly to let themselves go. Certainly he could not talk as he did and think her something other than she was—whatever she was—and why indeed should one not be anything, after all? At least that little bit of freedom could not be denied one. A rage existed in her tenderness for him. Why did he hold back to tantalize her? If he would kiss her perhaps she could force him to give her a taste of what it was she wanted of him. Why did such leches come to her? She didn't know a thing about what he was; what he thought, felt; where he came from.

It was two in the morning when they returned to the rooming house after having dined and danced. By this time Hilda was sure of her ground, even had there not been the recklessness of champagne gaiety to make her less careful, she was sure from the way he danced with her that she could achieve her will. As they came into the house she said:

"I don't understand you at all. You don't say a thing that will let me. Why won't you say more of yourself?"

"I bore myself to talk about, but what can I say to make you understand me if it's worthwhile doing that."

They went to her room and had soon retired. Files watched Hilda from the bed as she was removing her make-up before joining him. She was coolly matter of fact. It would have wearied him had she wished to indulge in sentimentalities. Women who wished affectionate caresses when he was scarcely moved physically by them always made him ill at ease.

As she joined him, Files felt relieved.

At any rate, the thing would be accomplished without romantic conversation. The contact of her cool body gradually warming against him did, however, arouse its pulsation of desire. Her caressing response was light. The slender hands tenderly over his face and body, submerged the too conscious so that he forgot to think.

Hilda breathed with sobbing breath of neurotic pain. After they had been together for several minutes and were tranquil, she whispered:

"I wonder if you realize how painful this is to me?"

"You mean you'd rather it didn't happen?"

"Of course not. Only it is agony. I don't know what you do to me. And do you care at all? . . . but don't answer. People like us should never ask questions like that of each other. I know the moment-after, and the day-after, aversion that can set in. Perhaps you dislike me now, and perhaps it will pass tomorrow. Sex is everything. Everything." She kissed him and took his mouth wholly to breathe as one with him. He felt a gratitude that she understood and was not too insistent that he talk. Now that the physical emotion had passed there was little feeling within him. A part of him she did understand, as he could understand a part of her, but he knew that they weren't for each other, not to continue through a long period. Yes, sex was too much everything; the hunger and demand for it; and the ideal of satisfaction for it that he was sure was never to be realized. Coldly his mind wanted him to have a feeling of sympathy, but it was not there for all that. He kissed her wondering if she too was simply being kind. The taste of her breath was pleasing; chemical—sandal wood, tamarac—acrid rather than too animal.

"You are wonderful when you kiss me so," Hilda told him. "As if the act were not all, and as if you had some feeling when that is done with. I oughtn't to ask it, but . . . don't answer if you don't wish, just stay quiet like this and don't speak—but do you want our relationship to become one that lasts some time. There are so many passing episodes for people like us. For you I'm sure. I felt that by the first sentence you spoke to me."

"O yes. We aren't the sort who surrender ourselves enough to be really lovers. I detest the possessive, combative tangle of mate relationships, and people who act as we, rather than as I, but of course sex can't be as impersonal as I want it."

"I understand too well. Will there never be anything lasting and dependable?"

"I envy no relationship I've ever seen. The solved thing in that case is too often demoralizing to one person or the other. One vamps on the other, or breaks the other in an attempt to possess completely. If there could be equality it would be all right, but why waste energy looking for that?"

Hilda pressed her body firmly to him, saying: "Bless you. I know we're friends through just what we know that so many won't know. We neither of us could be faithful, but I possess no jealousy any longer, and no vanity either. I've liked too many rotters to believe it a compliment when I myself attract somebody."

"I'm not that free. I can cover and conceal," Files answered, "but I can be burned out inside with jealousy too. The vanity I don't possess, because people who want me that I don't want anger me with any attention they give me."

"Do I bother you? Do tell me."

"No, you don't seem to be wanting to devour me. It's simply my appetite, and your appetite, and we're ready to be makeshifts to each other in that way. You don't represent the carnal thing at all to me, but I don't feel you trying to swallow my identity."

"I adore you; just that way. There are no demands on either side. We don't need to have scruples about each other."

"Just because of fear of what the other might feel. No. We needn't think in terms of scruples for each other. And with the ones who demand more and cling more we can be sympathetic so long as we care, and when we no longer care we'll be cold and not too scrupulous. There can't be kindness when its about sleeping with those one no longer desires."

In the morning Hilda awakened Files after coffee had arrived. She kissed him with a business-like "Bless you. How quietly you sleep. Almost not breathing."

Three minutes later her voice was again speaking, but now, her mind occupied with how to arrange her day, it was insect-dry, wind-driven, forced to re-iterate conversation. "My dear Files, what shall I do? I really must be leaving Berlin in a few days. How I will miss you, but we shall meet again. But I don't know what you feel. You're so silent. Do you even like me? You seem to have collected yourself together so much more for going on than I ever seem able to."

Files was uneasy. Hadn't he told her last night? He couldn't talk about his emotions when they were so indifferent. "We'll have dinner together tonight, won't we?" he asked, to evade her question.

"Do you ask? I thought that was understood."

"Do you mind if I ask that girl, Steve Rath, to come along? She'll leave after dinner, you can be sure."

"Not if you wish," Hilda answered, her voice sharp with question. "But why do you wish that?"

"Simply because she doesn't know what to do with herself in Berlin, and does damn fool things with the desperation of her loneliness. She's likeable, sober."

A sound of belligerent voices came from the hallway, and Files, being dressed, went to the door to see what was their source. He found it to be Steve in an argument with the landlady, who looked more than usually bedraggled this morning. Steve was obviously intoxicated, and the landlady certainly had taken a good share of cocaine within the last hour.

"This old hag thinks she is going to make me pay twice the price I agreed on for my room," Steve explained to Files, who took up the discussion for her, since his sobriety and his German were superior to hers. The landlady calmed down when aware that her threatening tone, as of blackmail in the offing, did not frighten the two auslanders, and she became apologetic when Files assured her that he might turn in a complaint about her room charges, which were above what the authorities allowed. It was known that she had never registered her house as a rooming place. After the scene, Steve said:

"I had my cases packed, but she wouldn't let me take them, the old thief."

"Where are you going?" Files asked.

"Back to France. I want to get by the seaside and cut out the booze."

"Good-bye, then. I'll be in France myself in a few days. We may encounter again," Files answered. When he returned to Hilda's room, she, having heard the conversation, informed him that she would go to Paris herself the next day. "So we won't stay out late tonight. Berlin doesn't attract me at all. But we shall meet in Paris, surely. We must. If you would only come with me," her voice left the question of invitation free of insistence.

And Files, as he went down the street some minutes later, found that Berlin was oppressing him, and had oppressed him for days. Restlessness raged through him, so he too decided the following night would see him on his way out of Germany. There was still a day to decide where, but it would not be Paris. It must be somewhere quiet.

The

 ndefinite

H *untress*

Lily strode firmly into the kitchen and threw down her string of ducks. She knew her mother thought her unladylike qualities a bad example for her younger sisters, so did not boast now of having brought down more game than any of the men who had gone to shoot ducks at early dawn. "There's no use reminding you," Mrs. Root sighed, "but you look like a tramp woman. I must lay it at my own door, of course. I tried to bring you up properly, but blood will tell, and you have your father's blood in you."

"Your family were the real aristocrats, weren't they, mother?" Lily said drily, "but what about your Aunt Helga, and you did run away and marry dad? He may not be much of a gent, but he lets a person be." Lily took off her rubber boots, and went to her room. Since the birth of the new baby the year before, Mrs. Root had relapsed again into complaining, but now she complained at Lily more than at Ole.

When Ole came in he started to speak of what a good shot Lily was but Ebba's manner stopped him. Instinctively he knew that antagonism and jealousy existed between Lily and Ebba, mainly on Ebba's side. Ebba didn't like the new easy comradeship between Ole and Lily, and she suspected that Ole was drinking heavily again and that Lily drank with him. Lily openly declared that clinging-vine women got on her nerves, and her mother countered by accusing her of imitating her Aunt Helga.

"Who's better in your family, mother?" Lily asked. "I hope I have her stuff, and you know you admire her, if you are afraid of what she can say."

Ole avoided becoming involved in the generally silent antagonism between the women. Since Ebba's having belatedly become tenderly desirous towards him Ole had found that her devotion didn't matter so much that he didn't need his drink. He was settled into later middle age and accepted Ebba as a home commodity now. Her fragility didn't make him feel so awkward, and he had come to know that she hadn't thought so much of her once-vaunted Swedish home background. Lily was a comrade to hunt and talk farm management with. He hoped she might become a strong business woman like her Aunt Helga.

Lily understood too that Ole was a simple, tender-hearted man, with the gentleness which hereditary heavy drinkers often have. Having his own weakness he was easily shamed and little critical of others. He and Lily now joked about Ebba's stories of her father's grand estate. "Dat goes vor de old country," Ole said, over snuff, "but from your Aunt Helga I get it. Ve are more progressive on our little farm than your mother admits." Another weakness of Ole's, newly acquired, was his snuff-chewing, and he knew with fear that Ebba would object violently if she discovered that he had this habit. He didn't like snuff much, but a naughty desire to do things Ebba thought low class was in him, even when he did them in secret.

Upstairs, Lily found her cousin Helga packing her trunks for departure that afternoon. During the summer the girls had grown fond of each other, and Helga was the first person with whom Lily had any relationship approaching intimacy. Helga was slight, fawn-haired, and dainty. Lily, who cared not at all about fine clothes for herself, delighted in Helga's wardrobe. When the Chatauqua season was on she had been happily aware that Helga commanded admiration from Lansing townspeople. The highest compliment they could pay her was to think her one of the entertainers. Lily had never had an opportunity to know a woman of elegance, but she thought Helga elegant. She talked of Paris, of manner and style. Lily felt perturbedly restless, wondering about the outside world.

Changing from her hunting clothes, Lily offered to help Helga pack. "I'll miss you," she said. "You're the one person who has ever told me of great places, except mother, and her ideas are old-fashioned."

"Aunt Ebba gets sentimental about her old home because Uncle Ole is stolid. At first I thought he was brutal," Helga said.

"Dad brutal? No, no," Lily defended quickly, ashamedly fearing that Helga knew how much her father drank. "I guess I'm the only one that understands him, and he's quiet because mother scolds." Naïve with triumph, she added, "Mother gets jealous of how well he and I get on. She needn't. If she stopped scolding we'd tell her things. He's shy with you."

"I would give a thousand to have hair like yours," Helga said, distraitly. "That color is worth a fortune. Let it down and I'll dress it for you. I'll give you any one of my gowns you like. It's too bad you aren't an opera singer. You'd get all the attention just by being on the stage, with your looks and vitality."

Lily chuckled and tore her hair loose with a free gesture. "What would a thing my size do with your finery? There's no use trying to make me elegant." She seated herself, however, and let Helga brush her long yellow hair. A ten o'clock morning sun sent a bright beam of light across the room. From the barnyard came the smell of fresh hay. The quacking of ducks and geese, the grunts and squeals of pigs, and the twittering of birds sounded outside.

"I love the crackle of your hair," Helga mused, running

it through her palms. Lily saw the whiteness of Helga's fine hands against her own hair, in the mirror. "It's as lively as you are, Lily. Oh, I envy you. Being in the country makes me restless, but I won't be happy in New York either. Don't go to cities to stay long, ever. They aren't for you. You don't get bored and nervously nauseated here."

"I'm always restless," Lily said, petting Helga's arm. "I don't know what I'll do, but something has to happen for me. I won't marry a farmer, and mother and I will quarrel if I stay here. Dad tells me she disliked her own mother. I have nothing against her, but I'm the sort who ought to clear out. It would be great to think I had a voice like you say, because I might have ambitions. But I just want without knowing what I want."

"I wish you could come with me," Helga said. "But I don't know what we'd do. Father lets me have money, but he wants to stay at his club. I can't stand being with Aunt Signe. You'd be miserable, trying to keep me from complaining."

"Don't worry about me," Lily boasted. "I'm no weak plant. Some days I know I'll be a great woman, but others I don't care."

"You're so strong. I feel like nothing beside you, but you make me feel vitality too. I don't cry defeat easily myself," Helga said.

"If you ever feel that way, let me know and I'll come and take care of you," Lily bragged. "I could do something even if dad wouldn't give me money. I can stand anything."

"Helga, the car's ready to take you to town," Ole Root called. Helga hastily shoved a few last things into her trunk and closed it. "Kiss me goodbye now, Lily. Everything will be rushed downstairs."

"Let me have a bit of your hair," Helga said. "It's the color I'll try if I ever have mine changed." She snipped off a length of Lily's hair and quickly put it into an envelope. "It's wonderful, having a cousin like you, who goes ahead. You always will. I'm afraid for myself."

Lily saw the look on Helga's face. She was trying not to weep. Lily felt cut with loneliness for her, and sad because she was sad. Then Lily broke away and bolted to her room. She wouldn't go downstairs to bid goodbye to Helga and have others see tears in her eyes. She stood at her window watching the car going towards town until it was out of sight.

2

Lily was in the yard beneath the umbrella tree. Her hair was loose and she stroked it musingly, liking the electric crackle, and thinking of how Helga had praised its color and gloss. Across the road from the farmyard thousands of yellow butterflies hovered over a late growth of uncut alfalfa. As she regarded them she saw them as a flood of flame rippling over the fields. If a lake of kerosene were set on fire it would appear that way, she reflected. Tranquility was deep within her. To look at the cattle standing in the marshes, lying in the pasture chewing their cuds, or moving lazily gave her full satisfaction. She wasn't artistic, she told herself, because she had no desire to paint pictures even had she known how. She was drily curt when her mother suggested that she go inside and get the churns ready for butter-making. That could wait. She'd get the butter made easily once she felt like beginning.

"May I have a drink of water, or buttermilk if you have

it?" a voice said. Somewhat resentfully Lily tossed her hair back and looked distantly out of chilled blue eyes at the speaker. He was Red Neill, who owned the restaurant in Lansing. Lily knew him only by sight, but remembered that he was one of the men who had been spoken of as a friend of Mrs. Watkins, when she had stayed with Mrs. Watkins two years back. He thought he was a real lady-killer, Lily surmised. Her pale eyes challenged his appraising glance with a glance more coldly appraising.

"There's the pump with a cup beside it and your hands aren't tied," Lily spoke curtly.

"You're not sociable this morning, Miss Root," Red said over his dipper of water. "I interrupted your toilette, I see, and I look pretty dirty with these ducks slung to me."

"That's not a bad string of ducks," Lily relaxed some. "I brought in more myself the other morning though. You're maybe a better hunter of other things than ducks."

"It's not all game that's worth the hunting," Red answered, "and what is, is scary sometimes. You never respond to my greetings in town. Perhaps you think I'm a bad one?"

"What would it mean to me if you were a bad one? I don't know you, and you only tried to speak to me because you thought I was one of Mrs. Watkins' kind. She's all right too, but I paid my board when I was with her, and stayed on because I wasn't going to let gossip bother me. I can be myself and as I want with whoever I am with."

Red shifted the ducks to his other shoulder. "I'll try and speak more respectfully next time, Miss Root," he said. "You deserve it. They don't make many like you in this part of the world."

"And what a favor you would do me! I may answer," Lily said, melting somewhat, and not wanting to believe stories about Red any more than she believed them about Mrs. Watkins. "I know it is girls you think are fine and elegant you really bother to be polite to. You have a fancy idea of yourself, I take it."

"You aren't meek yourself, Miss Root. But those others," Red's voice softened, "they have no blood in them. They don't feel anything."

Lily got red in the face and felt temper arise within her. "Pack your ducks on," she said sharply. "What blood or feeling you have doesn't interest me, and I'm busy."

After Red had gone Lily tried to believe she was in a temper at him, but she didn't believe so actually. She had seen rather surprised admiration in his eyes, and realized that he had wished to tease her too. She was resentful towards his patronizing attitude of male gallantry, which while appraising her didn't recognize that she was sizing him up too. She rather liked his ruddy, open face, but she resented his male coquettish attitude, and more, she believed he looked on her as a simple country girl who might be easy pickings, and susceptible to flattery.

Doing up her hair she still sat beneath the umbrella tree, tranquil, but restless too. An antagonistic feeling towards Red did not go out of her, but she imagined a romantic gallant who came upon a legendary herself while she was combing her tresses. The gallant was a mixture of Helga, Red, Dionisio Granger, and her father, but he had Red's curly, mahogany hair and athletic body. He was taciturn and mild like her father, but he had some look of painfully wistful beauty across his face which excited her. Lily, who wasn't given much to imagination or daydreams, found herself fancying a world peopled quite other than any world she knew, and as she had never read much, all her dream world's types were sublime examples of types she

had known in life. She was complicated, adjusting herself in this world of delicate and fragilely beautiful beings,
because she felt herself large, awkward, overgrown, and
horsy. She didn't, however, lose herself in her imagination. A pent-up rage persisted in her. People would think,
Mr. Neill had thought, that she was a buxom country
girl to be flirted with vulgarly. She concluded, though,
her resentment was not against Mr. Neill, or men's or
women's attitudes. It was against sex, and the importance
it assumes in people's lives. Except for a lazy tranquility
now in her, Lily would have been at this moment swept
with a sense of futility about life. The day was too lazy
for her to feel anything strongly though, but a despair
about action lived in her. She felt emptiness about her,
and realized that Helga too felt emptiness, while in cities
or travelling. Slumbering in Lily was an intense revolt
of rage at time, which is too generally dull. Life seemed
made of waiting for moments that were worth little when
they arrived. She resented Red Neill for being likeable
while a brutish quality in him antagonized her. She despised thinking of her mother's wail. About Ole she felt
gentle, but he answered nothing for her. Lily told herself
savagely if it ever came to a showdown she'd prove to
Red that she was stronger than he in every way. Again
she told herself she was silly to think she or Red were to
have anything to do with each other.

Dionisio Granger came into the yard carrying three
ducks, and Lily's heart plunged as she recognized him.
He was adolescent now, but quickly she saw he retained
the beauty which had cut into her. "You've been duck-
shooting, have you?" she asked, hoping he didn't sense
the panicky thrill in her.

"No, Red Neill gave me these," Dion said. "I went

hunting with him, but it made me feel rotten to see the ducks plop on the ground or in the water. I couldn't shoot straight anyway. Red pretended I hit some. He was going to give me more but I couldn't carry them."

"Why didn't he carry them all, the big husky?" Lily asked.

"I wanted to stop off and see Pete Simpkins at the next farm, and Red had to get back to town."

"He's a good-looking man, or dresses well," Lily conceded. "I like people who look trim. He won't get fresh with me as he thinks he can with most girls in town though. I guess he thinks I'm another foolish country girl while he's a high-class gentleman."

Dion sat on the grass beside Lily. "Red came into town a hobo not many years ago. He was one of those wandering newspaper fellows, a drunk, I think. Sister says he's intelligent. He went with her for a while, but she didn't want to go with him after she found out what other girls he hung around."

"He means nothing to me," Lily said. "Your sister's a real lady, the most beautiful I ever saw. I met her this summer with my cousin, but she didn't notice me. She never asked me to call like she did Helga. I'm too big a cow."

"No, she likes you," Dion said. "She thinks you're handsome, but thought you hated tea parties. I'm drowsy. I'm going to nap on the grass before I walk on to Simpkins'. You wake me if I really sleep." Dion rolled over to bury his head in his arm. The sunlight through the leaves got into his eyes. Lily saw how his brown hair grew around his ears and the back of his neck. It made her yearn towards him and hurt her by seeming so beautiful.

"Put your head on my lap and nap," she said, in terror that Dion might be shy, and not do as she suggested.

She placed his head on her lap, however, and stroked his hair once, to let her hand rest caressingly around the back of his dome. "I wanted to kidnap you two years back, did you know that?" she said, huskily tender with fear. "I nearly died, you looked so marvellous one day."

Dion blushed and laughed into her face. He felt a tingle in him because of her caress. She was vibrantly alive. He didn't nap, but stirred uneasily. "I'll get you some apple cider. It's hard and will make you gay," Lily said. She went to get the cider, and Dion did not feel like napping anymore. Soon he said he would have to go. "I'll walk to the end of the orchard with you," Lily said.

As they walked through the orchard Dion put his arm about Lily's waist until she laughed with contralto irony. "You little devil, Dion, do you want the countryside to be saying I rob the cradle? You'll be a real swell when you grow up, but you won't fall for a lump of meat like me. You'd snicker to think I was your first love."

"You're not fat," Dion said gravely. "Nobody looks at you once without looking again. Sis says that if you bothered about dress people would discover you as a beauty."

"It's hell, Dion. I don't know what to do with myself. I can't stay on the farm. I like fine people around me. But I need the country to turn around in." Lily was gaily melancholy.

Dion's arm pressed her waist. Quickly she stopped, put her arms about him to draw him close and kiss. "If you were older, I'd do things that weren't careful, but I'd scare you. You don't know how strong inside I feel about you. It's that you're beautiful, and maybe you won't always be. I have to have beautiful things or I won't live." Quickly she ran down the path. She would not turn to wave good-bye. She was afraid she had frightened Dion, or that he would think her a common, vulgar country girl. It hurt to think he wouldn't understand how sweetly she felt about him, with agony in the feeling. She was ashamed too to have teased him when he put his arm about her. His gesture had been smallboy companionable, as though he sensed and wished to comfort the desolate restlessness in her.

3

"Sure, Dion, you shot at least five ducks, but I'll send some of mine to your mother when we get back to town," Red Neill said. "This is the last hunting I'll have this season, and I'm taking a week in the city. This town has me run ragged. You've become a swell shot in three weeks." Red was garrulous, and perplexed at his own desire to please this Granger boy.

"Maybe I brought some down when we shot into that flock," Dion said earnestly. "Anyway, I don't feel sick seeing the ducks fall like I did. It got me seeing them fly as though nothing could stop them, and then they fall and are clean dead."

Dion felt sleepy. It was not nine o'clock, but Red and the three other men had shot all the ducks they wanted. Dion felt uncomfortable because Ike Sorenson joshed him. When the men began to get drunk he felt scary. Red cursed Jake Isaacs for offering the kid a drink, and Dion felt protected, but scared of Red's savagery towards Jake, Red saw. It made him shy with Dion. Red knew the Grangers had high ideas, and regretted having told Dion to lie to his mother about the number of ducks he had shot. He didn't want the boy to think him crooked, and he couldn't be scornful of Dion's goodie ideas as he was about most people's. Like his sister, Dion had a naïve gravity and a confidingly reticent manner. He seemed entirely trustful, but Red saw him look in wondering analysis at the others now and then. There was a quality of hurt wonder in him. Like his sister again, Dion was more apt to venture than most boys in town. The Grangers had real class, Red knew. He didn't know how to get at them.

Going across the fields the hunters scared up several coveys of prairie chicken at which they shot carelessly. By noon they stopped at farmer Matson's for lunch, after which they sat drinking with the old man. Red was morose, and swore at his companions. He was contemptuous of these hicks. Drink affected him that way, but he seldom got drunk. He was too aware of Dion's shy discomfort. He wanted to feel contemptuous of a too-delicate boy brought up by a protected mother, but instead he found himself gently understanding that the boy would be scared among lowbrows getting stinking drunk. He moved to sit nearer Dion, and started to put his arm comfortingly about the boy's shoulder, but he was afraid of frightening the boy. Dion didn't look scared so much as he looked wistful and lonely, not happy to be with these roughnecks. To hell with duck-shooting, Red thought. Why should Dion think it fun when he hated the sight of blood and couldn't help that feeling in himself?

Taking another drink Red obeyed his impulse to put his arm about Dion's shoulder. The boy was unrelaxed in his arm. "You're a great hunter," Red said, gruffly, ill at ease. "Forty ducks in three hours, you can tell your mother." Red was angry at himself for persisting upon telling Dion to lie about the number of ducks he had shot. He only wanted to help the youngster to prove he was a sort who could do things, but why didn't he get it into his noodle that Dion didn't care how many ducks he had shot, and that Dion always gravely assured him he wouldn't lie to his mother?

Dion fidgeted, conscious of Red's whiskey breath. "I couldn't fool her if I tried. I'll say you gave me the ducks."

"You're right," Red was elaborately placatory. "It doesn't pay to lie." Cursing himself as soon as he spoke he added, "Until you're old enough to know when you have to lie to dumb people."

Red's breath, and a sense of brutality in Red, made Dion move away, and he was afraid Red noticed. He couldn't lose the idea that Red had been a hobo, and he had further distrust he didn't analyze. However, he felt a furtive triumph in feeling that he was being much a man's man, with men who didn't treat him like a small boy.

Red pondered the Grangers. Why should they represent class to him? They weren't very rich and wouldn't have cut any great impression in a city. Yes, he had been a tough kid himself, but except that his mother was widowed she was as good class as Mrs. Granger. Unconsciously he put his arm about Dion again, and feeling the curve of Dion's shoulder in the palm of his hand he suddenly drew the boy to him. Dion looked up into his eyes, but his expression told nothing. Red didn't analyze, but he had a sharp terror. The boy's clear eyes told him nothing, but Dion's face swam before Red's vision with a beauty that made him dizzy. A moment later he realized that his sudden clutching at the boy may have frightened him. Dion, however, turned his head and smiled now. His eyes were limpidly clear, but Red knew Dion wanted to draw away. Red hated to have this boy think him brutish and drunken, and he hated his own coarseness. Right now Red knew that if the boy wanted anything, there was nothing he would not do to give it to him, but he suffered, knowing that Dion didn't care what he felt.

Red took a deep swig of whiskey. He felt a horrible desolation of life. Dion had him awed with terror by the unrevealing glisten in his clear eyes. There was no definite quality in their depths; not innocence, knowing, like, distaste; only wonder and questioning, but the questioning did not include him, Red knew. He wanted to think Dion liked him, but instead he feared Dion despised him more, if the boy had known his own feelings. The Grangers had a way of being sweetly well-bred with a tender consideration which annulled a person. If they hadn't that ethereal prettiness, Red told himself, he'd think them pampered snobs, but the look on Dion's face remained in his mind. He recalled that people suspected that old man Granger had suicided, and everybody but Mrs. Granger knew that her oldest son's death had not been an accident.

The look on Dion's face now showed that he was too abstractedly unaware of anybody's presence to care. Red wanted the boy to understand that he was a friend who would stick by him. As never before in his life Red wanted the sympathy he felt understood. It hurt him to think that the boy cringed from him, and from life, probably.

Thwartedly unable to express to Dion his wish to save him any misery, Red took another swig of whiskey. He hated it but finished off the bottle and threw it from him with a curse. He'd mucked around so much he couldn't even express a nice emotion anymore, and what had he ever gotten out of his lousy adventures that satisfied him, even momentarily?

"Do you know Lily Root?" Dion said, to break the silence. "She has come to town to live. She visited a cousin of hers in New York this summer and won't live on the farm. She surprised me, she's taken to dressing so well."

"Yes, nice girl," Red said distraitly, still wanting to remember Lily clearly since Dion mentioned her. She was that big Swede girl who always antagonized him. She had hair and eyes, he remembered from having come upon her while she was drying her hair last autumn. She gave herself airs because her father was a rich old penny-snatcher. "She might make the grade better than some skirts in town," he conceded.

"She's a real looker now," Dion said, "but she doesn't know what she'll do. She didn't like New York, and she doesn't like Lansing, or the farm."

"Hell, I ought to marry her," Red joked. "I'm getting on and ought to settle down and have kids. She'd make a good cowmother and keep house for me. She's about the rate for a roughneck like me, since I gave up my fancy idea of falling for your sister. It was damnfoolishness. I'm loose as hell. She was right, not to see me for dust."

"Were you really a hobo, the way people say?" Dion asked. His intimate tone made Red desire to talk of his life, to make the boy understand that he wasn't a real lowbrow.

"I'll tell you, Dion," Red said. "My old man croaked when I was a kid, and mother had no money. I don't know what happened to my older brother, and I started to drift when I was sixteen. I worked in a newspaper office and was a reporter, but after I got back from France I didn't feel like taking any work I could get. I bummed around for a couple of years, sort of de luxe. When I hit town and saw your sister, I decided to stay. Later I had a chance to get my restaurant. I decided life was as much here as anywhere, and I sold real estate, and now you see the Honorable Mr. Neill, one of Lansing's foremost citizens. I haven't been crooked, Dion. I had luck and made money. There's lots I could tell you, but I'm not a cheap tough like some people in town think. I don't toady to most of the church-going people, so I hang around with whoever there is to be with. It isn't my fault they're cheap. I can stand cheap skirts, but with men who are lowbrows I want to fight when I drink, and you know I drink."

"Did you really want to marry Neva?" Dion asked.

"I didn't think," Red mused. "She got me, that was all. I sort of felt she'd break if I touched her. She scared me, that was it. Now I figure I was as good as that husband she has. Knowing you don't like him is the only reason I'd let on what I think of him."

"He's just dumb," Dion said. "If Neva had known what a tightwad he was she wouldn't have married him. In college he seemed lively, she says, but he claims he has to be a church pillar if he's going in for politics in this town."

"I'd make a hell of a husband for a delicate woman. It's best she wouldn't have me, I guess," Red said.

It was late afternoon before the men were back in town. "Stick around," Red said to Dion. "Ma Jensen will cook us some ducks. I'll have my nigger carry yours back to your mother."

Ma Jensen waddled out of the City Restaurant kitchen. "Ay tink ve giff de poys a goot feed, all vor de same moneys," she commented with sturdy satisfaction, her face shiny from kitchen heat as she felt the breasts of the ducks.

"Sure, and ma, give any hoboes who come around a handout. No use having the game spoil on us," Red said carelessly. He didn't feel morose now; he felt elation, planning to take the midnight train to Minneapolis. Feeling the bristles on his face he went upstairs to shave. When he came down he looked well-groomed. Ma Jensen saw that he was in a mood again, which meant he'd take the train to the city. "Dot is pad vor pizness," Ma mumbled to the second cook. She didn't trust the cashier. "Sooch a svell guy you is," she complimented Red. "Choost like a traffeling man."

Red grinned and patted Ma's fat shoulder, amused at her busy waddlings, her Norwegian mixture of thrift and generosity, and her garrulousness. Ma loved talk, and being talked to. Red wondered where Dion was until he saw him across the street with some swell dame. It might be one of his older sisters home on a vacation. The Granger girls all had class, and the two older ones who lived in Chicago were not stuck-up, or afraid of towns-people's opinions. They were sure of themselves, know-ing that girls in town were apt to copy their style. Red was impressed by them, but he resented the older one who had sold Neva on that freedom-of-women business. Red granted that she had a mind, and he didn't blame her for giving most men the laugh, but all the same, he argued, it's men who supply the world's brains. Red had tried to give her an argument once, but she snowed him under, mentioning books, and quoting people he had never heard of. She claimed they were big noises, and he couldn't prove different.

Red went across the street to get Dion and talk to his sister, if it was a sister. Red was shy. She might wonder why he was horning in, or if he was being an evil influ-ence on her kid brother. Red was restless. He needed a trip to Minneapolis, to cut loose for a couple of weeks.

Red saw that the girl with Dion was large, firm-bodied,

and stalwart in a way unlike any of the Granger girls. She was handsome though. "You don't recognize me, Mr. Neill," Lily Root said. "We're both better dressed than the last time we met, that's the truth."

Red didn't show his surprise. He had always thought Lily a big, healthy, strong-bodied farm girl, with keen eyes and startling hair, but now she looked somebody, and had a poised manner. A faint scent came to Red's nostrils, and it was not cheap perfume. That swell cousin of hers had probably taught her a few things. Still Red appraised Lily as a big girl who would go well in a leg show where they want big women who can show much white flesh and yellow hair. He heard her laugh, and its timbre left a voluptuous taunt in his ear. There was a quick flashing light, of gold gleaming tawnily, in the blue of her eyes when she glanced at him. A forbidding antagonism he had sensed in her once was not now present. It pleased Red to think that Dion had perhaps put her less on her guard, which meant that the boy liked him well enough to praise him. "Dion told me you were in town," he said.

"Yes, I can't stand the farm after a few months in the East. If dad can't give me money to stay in town I'll have to go to work. Maybe I can start a dressmaking business, if there are enough women in town to buy fashionable clothes."

"With your style you won't have any trouble getting on." Red was complimentary. Lily was striking him as femininely alluring and poised, rather than as a mere husky country dame. Maybe he had never taken a good look at her before. As she talked the situation became social, and Red found himself wanting to impress her with conversation rather than just kidding her along. He had a feeling that he spent so much time joshing waitresses and tough Janes in town that he had forgotten how to talk straight to a woman with class.

"I'll manage. It's probably that I'm changing, but my father seems to be a tightwad and I have two sisters and a small brother who have to be brought up. I'll have to manage on my own. If I'd known earlier I'd have educated myself more, but I don't want to be a stenographer or a schoolteacher either," Lily talked, somehow consulting Red, or assuming that he would understand her situation and offer advice. Red surmised that she had heard he'd made money off real estate, and had decided she might make a go at him. The idea of marrying a large woman like Lily struck Red as funny. He had always liked them slender and graceful, and Lily was six foot tall, broad-shouldered, and while handsomely proportioned, her size made one think she could walk through stone buildings, and she had a way of progressing as though she meant to get where she was going.

Boys were playing baseball in the street, and one of the throws caught Dion full in the face so that he toppled over. Red saw, and thought the boy was unconscious. Dion was dazed when Red helped him to his feet. "Are you hurt much?" Red asked. "Don't rub your eye. We'll have the doctor see to that right away. He's going to be sick." Red held Dion anxiously, patting his shoulder and feeling enraged at the boys who were playing fly-catch.

"It will be all right in a few minutes," Dionisio said, pushing away from Red, preoccupied with the pain in his eye. "It got me straight over the eye, but it wasn't coming fast. I've been socked in the eye harder than that, but it drove the ball in. I feel woozy and sick in my stomach. I'm going home. No duck dinner for me."

Lily watched with concern. Red's gentleness towards

Dion struck her, and affected her strangely. She had decided not to act antagonistic towards him, but still she believed him without gentleness in his nature. There was some luminously tender quality in his treatment of Dion. Lily felt resentful. "I'll walk home with you, Dion," she said, "because you might feel sick and want somebody to hold you up."

"That's all right," Red said gruffly. "I'll take him home in the car. We don't want anything wrong with his eye though. Come on, Dion. We'll have the druggist take a look at it and if it's inflamed, we'll see the doctor." Red had his arm about Dion's shoulder, and pulled the boy around, to lead him towards the pharmacist's. Lily was in his path. She hesitated, and took Dion's other arm.

"Yes, you're right," she told Red. "We'd better see that his eye isn't in danger."

Red sensed that Lily was challenging him. He felt a desire to be rude and tell her that Dion was his friend to look after. She needn't think he meant harm to the boy. Lily's calm, however, cowed him. Let her take Dion home. At the drugstore Mr. Schwarz made light of the blow on Dion's eye.

"It'll be all right in a half hour. The ball wasn't coming fast enough to blacken your eye, sonny."

"I know, but I'm going home. Don't bother," Dion said, petulantly. He didn't like being fussed over, and his eye felt as though it had sand in it. He broke away from Red and Lily now and went down the street. As the druggist had washed his eye and he looked healthy colored they let him go on alone. When he had left Lily looked strangely at Red. "You aren't as tough as I thought you were. I never thought you'd feel hurt for anybody else's hurt. Maybe I act harder than I am too." There was a wistful warmth of appeal in Lily's voice at her last admission. She laughed, nervous because of having been personal. Red felt a fondly human impulse towards her.

"Too," he said, and laughed uneasily. "Yes, you and me both. I'm not hard. I'm not so gentle, but I don't like seeing a nice kid's eye put out, I don't care who the kid is."

"Oh, I know," Lily said quickly. "I saw. You wouldn't be so bothered by every kid who got hit in the eye. I have nearly kidnapped Dion myself, twice. There he is, and suddenly he looks so beautiful it kills a person. I never thought you would be able to appreciate that kind of look on a person's face."

Red looked confused, as well as surprised. "What do you mean?" he said gruffly.

"Let it go," Lily's voice chortled a tender mocking lilt. "Anyway, I like you a little now; not the way you are acting, but how I see you really are. Maybe I placed too much importance on what people said about you."

"What do they say?" Red asked sullenly.

"Things about your attitude towards women, and Dion says his mother thinks you may give him bad ideas. I told Dion if his mother thought he wouldn't learn things from farm boys and other people in town, she had another think coming. What town people think they can get by with in the country riles me."

"You don't like this burg any better than I do," Red said.

"No, but I get lonely in the city and don't know what to do with myself. I don't want to stay on the farm because I've come to feel restless and get cross with the others. I guess this town is where I'll stay."

"I'm going to Minneapolis on the midnight train. Why not come along?" Red said, with a drummer-like gallantry of implication. He saw Lily flush resentfully. "I didn't insinuate anything," he defended.

"No, you were honest enough. You said it outright."

"I didn't suggest anything."

"Don't be foolish. What right would I have to go with you if I didn't understand it the way you know you meant it?"

"Well, you told me Dion's family thought I wasn't fit to know," Red hedged, uneasy now. He didn't understand Lily. She kept changing before him. There she stood, seeming a healthy, knowing farm girl, very physical, and at moments he got the feeling he had to be more careful about what he said to her than he had with the Granger girls. She wouldn't kid or joke about herself. Just now there was a stark, raw quality of blunt and very young honesty in her attitude towards his suggestion.

In her remark upon his tenderness towards Dion there had been a teasingly sympathetic woman of the world's understanding. Then Red felt that she outthought him, and understood more than did he. He knew he was not of a subtle or delicate sort.

"I said they might be mistaken. Maybe I was wrong, but let that drop. I don't accept your invitation, thank you, however you meant it. I have a man's way of looking at things, and if I went I'd want my own money, and I can't afford a trip to the city just now, if I wanted to go with you. We would probably want to do different things there, so we wouldn't be company for each other anyway."

Red laughed. "You're some girl, Miss Root. You have a different line than any other skirt I ever talked to. I say, you eat Dion's duck dinner with me, and we'll go for an auto ride afterwards. I won't act fresh."

Lily became somewhat defiant. "I'm no weak woman. Certainly I'll eat with you, and we might talk sense. If you talk to me and treat me as though I don't think as much of myself as you do of yourself, I can leave, I suppose."

At dinner Lily was on her guard for a time, but mischief came into her. She found she wasn't at all distrustful of Red. Instead she felt surer of herself than he did of himself. "Why would you want me to go to the city with you?" she asked. "That was an idea which would have worried you if I'd accepted, isn't it? You have girls there, I know. You grew up in the city, didn't you? We don't know a thing about each other, so we don't get at each other when we talk, do we?"

Red mumbled and wanted to draw within himself because Lily manipulated the situation rather than he. "There's not much to know about me. I was a bum newspaperman, and a hobo after I got back from the war. Another fellow put me wise to the fact that I could buy this restaurant cheap, and when I saw Neva Granger I had ideas about settling down, and this town looked as good as anywhere else. She's not so good-looking now, with two kids, but I fell hard then. I guess she was meant to be just refined. Anyway, when she heard about my being drunk a few times she was through with me, and I pulled what she thought was a crooked deal getting hold of a couple of farms. One man had consumption and had to get away quick; the other fellow was bankrupt. I hadn't much money, but managed to borrow and buy the farms, at different times, but she decided I was no good. It wasn't any good my telling her that I sent that T.B. guy money every month, and have for five years. She wouldn't believe it, and I guess she was right to marry that rosy-cheeked nice boy she has."

Lily mused. "Both the younger Granger girls and Dion have something that upsets a person. The one you liked isn't so pretty now, but three years back I used to feel sick about myself, seeing both her and the other girl. I felt like a load of meat. My mother was beautiful in that dainty, delicate way, but you couldn't tell it by looking at me. I don't know why, I never wanted to be that way, still I like looking at girls who are beautiful their way. It's funny too, because Dion's that way, and he isn't girlish. It's just that they are beautiful, and it hasn't anything to do with their being girls. Oh, I haven't enough education to express what I feel, but it's poetical, I suppose." Lily said the last very youngly and for a flash was a crude, romantic farm girl. Before the last romantic admission Red had been bothered by her wondering about his devotion to the Grangers. She calmly assumed that he felt about them all, Dion included, as did she, and it disturbed him to think that she was right. He hated to have her know how keenly he felt about Dion.

Driving out into the country after dinner Lily was not talkative. Her quietness put Red off his guard, and he finally, in a wooded section of the road, tried to put his arm about her. She did not resist until he tried to caress her firm breast. She merely pushed his hand away and sat back. Red was nervous. His legs were jerky, and he felt restless, wishing he was on the train towards Minneapolis. He tried to tell himself that he had this girl going, and that he would tantalize her. A look in the depths of her cool eyes upset his calculations, however. She was warm and full-blooded. He was not going to believe that she was an iceberg and Swedes are all hot. She bothered him.

Her knowing Dion and the Grangers bothered him too. He didn't want her telling that he was a lousy roughneck. Moments of tiredness with the game he believed he was playing came to Red. Why bother with her? She was right. There were girls in the city, and maybe this girl did run straight. He might get into a jam playing with her. Her Swede father might have more money and influence than people in town knew. You could never tell about those Swede farmers. Still Red later tussled with Lily, to kiss her. She resisted only mildly.

"If you treated me the way you did Dion this afternoon you could do anything," Lily suddenly blurted out. "It struck me you were more hurt than he was when that baseball hit him. I knew then you weren't a tough man. I never saw anybody act so tender. Your treating me this way won't get you anywhere. I never did like being handled."

Red gulped and got red in the face. "Whatcha driving at?" he said gruffly.

"You make me want to be kind to you, because of how I see you can feel, but you don't let me be as much as I can be. I'd talk honestly to you, if you would, but if girls you know want being played with like this, I'm not like them, that's all. If I wanted to do anything, I would, but you act as though you thought you could play a trick on me and have things happen. I'm able to think too, remember." Lily's tones were not antagonistic though. They were confiding, cajoling, and, Red felt, somehow aggressive. He sensed that with a hunting and hard curiosity this girl was tantalizing and analyzing him.

He in no way understood how few contacts with people Lily had had in her life. Whatever she knew she had observed from a distance. Her alone childhood, her

early look of maturity because of size, and her mother's
mansion-lady attitudes towards farm neighbors had kept
her from intimate friendships on the farm, and away at
school her self-consciousness had stopped her.

Country quiet and new-cut grain odors were giving
Lily tranquility, but a feeling of indifference, or abandon,
also. She felt perplexed, for at dinner she saw that she had
attracted Red, and now he treated her with a familiarity
she thought cheap. Possibly that is how sex is, but she
didn't like having him start things. She felt drawn to him
whenever he looked helpless or confused, as she had managed to make him feel several times. She liked the feel of
him beside her now, but at this moment he seemed coldly
detached. She hadn't observed it acutely before, but seeing his hands on the steering wheel she saw that they were
finely made with very well-kept fingernails. A sensation
of desire went through her. She loved beautiful hands.
Seeing that Red's were fine made her appraise him more.
His straight shoulders and his strong, elastic body made
her feel the pulse of life keenly. Suddenly she patted his
arm, and then held it comfortingly in her hand.

"I get crazy blue and lonely sometimes too. Don't look
cut off from everything, and fighting about it. I'd be a
good friend to you, and just let it go at that if you'd take
things simply."

Red was uneasy. Lily attracted him more than he wanted
to admit, and he was incapable of taking her comradeship suggestion. Without distrusting her, he was on his
guard. She was aggressive in a strange way. He squeezed
her hand, trying to believe he thought he had her excited, but also he told himself she was one of those foreign freaks who don't have any passion or feeling. When
he pressed her hand Lily responded. He kissed her, and

she responded, but not passionately. Lily let him kiss her again, and patted his backhead with a comforting gesture. Red felt somehow timid, but forced to go on, to tussle when Lily's hand against his bosom kept him from crushing her to him. He saw that her strength was greater than his.

Lily drew away finally, saying, "You're afraid of me. Why? I know you don't feel anything much about me. You don't feel tender, anyway, and I guess you know I won't let myself be treated like you're used to treating some girls. Let me tell you, if anything happened between us it would be because I wanted it, but I don't want anything with you thinking I'm just another girl who's gone out for a ride in the country with you. When I do that it will be with someone I pick up and take out riding. I want to be liked." When Lily started speaking she had been antagonistic, but a dismal quality of desolation came into her voice. It clutched into Red. He saw Lily in a flash as a great lonely child, overgrown, and groping. And passion came into him too. "I want you," he said. "You want me. That's it. We want each other." He caught her in his arms and held her close. She did not fight, but let him kiss her deeply, with long kisses. Then slowly she forced him away.

"I'm stronger than you," she said drily. "That kind of kiss means nothing. I was ready to offer you something but you wouldn't understand."

"Some fellows would make you walk home," Red said roughly. Lily was quiet for a moment, looking at him with a stunned air. Then she laughed, tauntingly until real mirth of dismay was in her voice.

"They would have to be stronger than you are. I might put them out of the car and let them walk home. You're funny with your idea that because I'm a woman you can make me do anything I don't want."

Red looked at Lily. Her face was impassive. He thought her icy with fury. "Come now," he was placatory. "I didn't mean that. Don't get all het up."

"I don't understand why you make things bad that needn't be so," Lily said, with childish bitterness. "Drive to town. I'm sick of things, sick of the way people treat each other. I want things nice. You were nice to Dion, why don't you act so with me? When I stayed with Mrs. Watkins people talked about me when I didn't know what they meant at first. Whatever she does she does for money, I suppose. I can't see that she's worse than women married to men they don't like, but I don't understand women like her or most other women anyway. You think I'm a stupid farm girl, but you're only the Irish owner of a cheap restaurant. I have more to be proud of than you, because I don't try to make anyone cheaper than they are."

"Do you want me to offer marriage because I kissed you?" Red said gruffly, it dawning on him that Lily was young, and not as knowing as he had thought.

"Why would I want that when I wouldn't marry you? That would be no compliment to me," Lily said, but she had detected bewilderment in Red's manner. Possibly, she thought, he had known only the wrong sort of women, and men. "We might do as well as most married people at that," she said after a silence. "I wouldn't be a home woman, and I wouldn't stop doing what I wanted to do and thought right because I was married."

"I didn't want to marry till I could leave a little money if I passed out," Red said, blood panicking through him. He told himself this big girl was not his type; that she was being clever and leading him on; but he was afraid too she was as indifferent as she claimed to be.

"I have money," Lily said shortly. Suddenly she felt decisive. "Yes, I will marry you. I have a business head, father will help me stock a ranch, and I can raise horses or cattle. It will be better if I am married, because people won't think they can trick a simple, unmarried young girl then. I want to do something to keep from being bored and restless." There was in Lily's tone no doubt but that now she'd decided the marriage was arranged.

Red fidgeted and felt caught. Lily sensed his trapped emotion and felt sympathetic. It gave her a physical urge towards him and she felt his magnetism. Her wish to have him gentle had passed. She felt the bewildered, awkward maleness of him, and knew she wouldn't mind if he became rough towards her again. She knew she was handling the situation, and she felt protective towards him, even to the extent of wanting to let him feel the master enough not to feel beaten. His arm rested now about her waist simply. She put her arm about his shoulder to look at his face. She felt the sinuous flux of his muscle beneath her palm, and it made her desire to hold him closer. However, watching his face she saw mingled emotions expressed there: panic at being trapped, withdrawal, abashment, and still Red was feeling her presence keenly. She aroused his desires.

Lily wanted him to look her in the face. His profile struck her as beautiful against the moonlight, and she had her old marvel at the wonder of faces. She had too a keen, deep-thrusting emotion that Red had been up against a hard life, and she wanted to pet and comfort him. When she started to draw him towards her he was taut in her grasp, and curiously hunted in his expression. Red wondered if she intended to have him, to force him to marriage. Her aggressiveness made him wary. If she had him caught, she had him licked too, he knew.

Lily's arm slipped away. Red looked at her. She was apathetic, with a beaten, uncaring look on her face. "No, you're not my answer," Lily said. Red felt a pang of pity and sympathy for the cold distance in her voice. She was different. She was something real. He wanted her, by God, and she was slipping away if he didn't act quickly.

"Hell, Lily, let's get married. I don't know why you would want me. I'm not much, and the idea of marrying and being responsible for kids that might turn out bad, or not like the racket, has always put me off." Red was humble with reality now, feeling defeat about life. "I get sick of that damn restaurant, but I haven't much hope. You don't know what you want either. Let's give marriage a shot. We can quit if it doesn't go."

"I was ready to go ahead with you and didn't think about marrying. That doesn't solve anything," Lily said, gloomily. "You think I'm trying to force you into a marriage, and all I want is to know what's nice in you. I don't know people, I guess, and I don't like them much. I want things nice. You don't want to marry me, even if you don't manage to get the kind of a woman you really like."

"You ask Dion," Red became persuasive now that Lily held back. "I said today I ought to marry a girl like you and begin to have sense."

Lily was distant with a distraitness which was that of a wild but unafraid animal. She didn't want Red now, but wished rather to fight him off apathetically. "You're a wise Jane," Red insisted. "Say the word and we'll head towards the preacher's. You don't start things you don't finish. You aren't that sort."

"Don't call me a Jane," Lily said curtly. "Go to a minister's then. Maybe there's a little something between us, and we will stop antagonizing each other. I'm ready to try marrying, and if it doesn't go, I have my living to make, and we can each go on our own."

4

Red and Lily felt evasive towards each other the next day, but each regarded the other curiously when the other was not looking. Neither of them quite figured out how they happened into this impulsive marriage, and Lily felt that she had tricked herself. Red had been gentle, and she didn't feel any virginal resentment towards him. All antagonism had gone out of her towards him, but she didn't want marriage or him, she told herself. He was awkward or things were grotesque, and she felt in no way romantic about marriage or love or sex. She felt a sense of pity for him when Red introduced her to various men at lunch. His manner of pride was pompous and wished to conceal sheepishness as he said, "Meet Mrs. Neill." She wanted to laugh at the droll pathos of his manner, which was perplexed. At dinner that night she made an attempt to get things straight.

"Red, do you want to go on? We are not what each other wants. We could call it quits now; go to the city and I'd stay there, and when I came back after a few months, just let the whole matter drop."

"What's the trouble, girl?" Red said, believing it needful to be a conventional and possessive husband with patronizing protectiveness. "Am I too rough for you? I thought you knew more than you do."

"It's not that," Lily said. "We didn't want marriage. We

bluffed ourselves into it. We ought to love each other a little if we stay married. I suppose I'm funny. I've been in love with Dion Granger for two years, somehow. I don't want him like what you did last night, but I get arm hunger and want him to pet whenever I think of him. I want to feel something that way towards anybody who's making love to me. That other doesn't mean anything to me."

"Well, I won't bother you. You wait a while and maybe in a few days you will feel differently," Red told her. "I know some women have to take things easily."

"I don't hate it, but I only felt sorry for you, and I won't go on feeling sorry all the time. I would just want you away. I tell you now, you don't ever need to be faithful to me that way, because if that's what you want, I'm no good for you. Maybe if you treated me or felt for me as you did yesterday for Dion things would be different, but you don't think my being hurt matters much, really."

"Ya, I get you," Red said gruffly, looking strangely at Lily. "You think I feel about Dion as you do, that's it?"

"I thought you and I had something between us maybe, in understanding how he can get a person."

"We might as well stick to the marriage for a while though, I say. I was going to Minneapolis. I'll go today, and you take care of the restaurant. You say you can manage and want to do things. When I get back you will have had time to think things over."

"All right," Lily said, a new idea making her eager. "That's so. We could stay married, and if things don't go I can go into some business of my own or raise stock. I guess I'm the kind of a woman who ought to be in business anyway. I'm no homebody."

Within a month Lily completely managed the restaurant. When Red came back from the city he paid more attention to farms and bare land which he owned. He opened a real estate office, and was soon asking Lily's advice about all his affairs. Ole, a rich man actually, was pleased that Lily should want to become a stock raiser and business woman as his staunch and independent aunt in Sweden was. He gave Lily blooded beef cattle, and horses, and daily she drove to the farm of Red's where she reared her stock.

Red, having married, believed he wanted children, but none arrived, and Lily's attitude towards him did not alter to make her desirous of him. She confused him entirely, for he had a deeply rooted conventional and male attitude towards women and marriage. Strangely he felt faithful towards her, even when she submitted so indifferently to his few efforts at love-making. He drank more heavily, and, always inclined to laziness, sullenly admired Lily's energy and business capacity, while letting her take his affairs more and more into her charge. He watched with strange emotions one day as she was regarding her blooded horses on the farm. There was more between her and the horses than there was between her and him, or her and humans. Later, one of his increasingly brutish and sullen streaks came over him, and he cursed her horses, which she gave more attention than she gave her husband.

Lily looked at him coolly. "Why, Red, you aren't jealous of my horses. We agreed to make the best of a makeshift marriage that neither of us wanted, but I have played square."

Red didn't answer. Lily, for physical strength and for surety of attitude, was the stronger. There was no use in his trying to bully her. She won; and the amiable, lazy streak in him led him to acquiesce finally with grace. Still, one time when Lily was at the farm for three days, nursing her pet Arabian stallion, Red was disturbed. What kind of a woman was she? She treated that horse more lovingly than most mothers treat their children. He was sure that should the horse die it would be a tragedy to Lily.

Abab, the stallion, was well soon, however. Red drove out to get Lily, and came into the farmyard to find her putting Abab through his paces. He pranced daintily, coyly exhibiting his sweeping tail and arched neck. After circling about Lily, who directed him by his halter lead, he pranced gracefully to her, and elegantly took a lump of sugar from her lips. Lily stood patting his glossy neck, before the stable man led him away to groom.

"Lily, you're a girl all choked up with protective emotions, and not a womanly or motherly impulse," Red said suddenly, bitter, but with a flash of insight rare to his mediocre nature. Lily looked abstracted.

Several years after their marriage Dion Granger returned to town for the summer vacation from college. Meeting Lily, he complimented her on her happy marriage. Lily was preoccupied, remembering the emotion she had once felt about Dion. When she was sixteen, feeling herself an awkward hulk of a girl, she had been hopelessly in love with the twelve-year-old boy, and terrified both that he should know or that he might not understand. Dion still had a quality that got into her, but her heart did not thump at his approach. She was wondering what quality it was she wanted and now felt that she was missing in life. Her farms, her stock, her business enterprises were not enough. Absent-mindedly she answered Dion. "Yes, Red and I are like lambs together. We don't row at each other. He likes being lazy, and I like doing things. Sure, it's a good marriage."

Seeing Lily talking at various times with Dion, Red recalled her confession of regard for the boy. He pondered, at first thickly suspicious and inclined to be jealous, but after reflection he spoke to Lily. "If you feel the way you do about that boy," Red did not call him Dion now; Lily's attitude made him feel estranged, as did Dion's added age, "I guess it's up to me to be a sport. Seeing how, you say anyway, we bluffed each other into this marriage, and don't mean much to each other . . . well, he's too young to marry you, but he likes you, and you're a strong, healthy woman. I just want you to get what I'm driving at." Red was embarrassed and ill at ease, as he mumbled.

Lily regarded him analytically. "It's not Dion. It's a quality he has. I once wanted what you're talking about, but not now, and I only wanted to hold him and comfort him. It was arm hunger. He seemed so fragile, needing to be taken care of. I know you'd mind, Red. You'd be jealous, several ways, if you thought I made a go at him, and it would have to be me. He doesn't understand. You have ideas that all women want the same thing, Red, but I tell you, I don't, and I don't understand myself any better than you do."

The next autumn Red went duck-shooting but once. With each year he grew lazier and less inclined even to hunt, his favorite pastime. Having drunk much whiskey, Red got a chill coming home in a heavy rain. He thought he would be well in a few days, but pneumonia set in and within five days he was dead. Lily felt dumfounded and empty. With Red about, she felt pride in proving to him how competent and fair a person she was. Their relationship had been an easy, sporting comradeship, she felt. To keep from being lonely she went further into stock raising. Constantly she drove about the country, looking for bargain lands or blooded stock to buy. She had become a woman of importance in the town and county now, because of her business ability and wealth. There was little of the lumpish girl about her now. For a time she was too busy to feel restless or to question whether she was happy. Only she felt a drive within her that insisted that she must not stop to wonder about herself. One day, in a fit of memory and curiosity, she wrote to her cousin Helga, from whom she had not heard for several years.

That day a mood of depression had her. In her restaurant she confided to her attorney, who lunched there daily, that there never would be another man like Red. Going into her room that night she looked at his photographs, and felt a pain of yearning. He had had moments of striking her as beautiful, or wistful. A sinking sensation came into Lily. The photographs swam before her eyes, and sometimes they suggested Red, but they became again Helga, and Dionisio, and even Abab, her pet stallion. In all of the heads was a nervously intense quality, a line of beauty which struck into Lily's heart and made her bleed for their torment and emotions of despair.

She was overcome with misery, feeling empty and nauseated in a vast unawakened realm of herself. What was she missing in life? Was she strong? As strong as Helga, and was Helga happy, or perhaps needing her? That night she dreamed of Dion, but in the dream he changed to Red, to Helga, to a horse, which became again Red, and she and Red were running up the sky. With a snap she felt herself falling into eternity, and awoke, startled, with a stale terror and sense of misery.

Upon awakening in the morning Lily felt so nauseated in the pit of her stomach that she went to see a doctor. He told her she needed a change and a rest. She had overworked and was due for a nervous breakdown if she did not relax. She overrated the physical resistance of her apparently healthy frame.

"Perhaps I do need change. There are qualities in the world I don't know. I might travel, and find out about them. Fortunately Johnson, my farm manager, can look after my affairs if I stay away even a year."

Lily didn't act at once, however. Nobody in Lansing attracted her, and she hadn't many friends, merely business acquaintances. Still she knew Lansing, and a fear of new places was in her. Helga was married, and had children, so that Lily felt that she would be intruding should she write that she was coming to New York for a visit.

She tried to feel what she hungered for, to reconstruct some picture of Red in her mind to which she might remain loyal. That might calm her. She was too emotionally upset and honest now to trick herself, however. It wasn't Red's kind of quality that ever had or could move her. Dion, as a boy, had meant strange, thrilled, frightened emotions. Helga's fragility she had worshipped. Somewhere there must be people or qualities which meant similar ecstatic emotions.

Helga responded at once to Lily's letter, and Lily, knowing the handwriting, opened the letter with hands trembling with expectancy. This letter was going to solve things for her. She knew before she had finished the first sentence, and was triumphant, with a new purposefulness. Always she had wanted to have Helga with her, to take care of and protect. She had been a child not to have known before.

"Darling Lily: You said that I should come to you if I felt utterly without will to go on. I feel so now. My husband is living with another woman, and accuses me of being silly and hysterical. He has never meant anything to me, nor have the children, much. I must get away. I want so much to come to you for rest, and to adjust myself. You are so confident and strong. Do you remember the hair I clipped from your head, years ago, it seems? I still have it, and it always reminds me that there is brightness and you. I'm too sick-hearted to write more."

Lily went with quick decision to wire Helga. "Coming to you at once. Lansing not for us, now. Plan a year abroad. We are saving each other."

As Lily left the post office after sending her wire she felt exuberantly young as she had not felt since childhood. Helga needed her. Helga, a person, felt she had strength beyond mere managing capacity. Helga meant a release into a human relationship, and Helga meant some mystery that was going to be solved for her now.

Encountering the doctor who asked when she planned going abroad Lily said gaily, "I'm on my way to packing, and will be on the train towards New York tonight. Doctor, it's good I have money, because I have a strong feeling I'm breaking loose to learn what living is about. If there's anything in life that matters, I'm going to find it. I've been compromising too long."

Ed Lorusso lives in Albuquerque, where he is finishing a doctoral degree in English at the University of New Mexico. He edited and introduced the UNM Press 1990 reprint of Robert McAlmon's *Village* and 1991 collection, *Post-Adolescence*. He also wrote the afterword for the reprint of *The One Who Is Legion* by Natalie Barney, reprinted in 1987 by the National Poetry Foundation, University of Maine. And he has written a novel, *Letters from Oblivion*, based on McAlmon's life and times.